Five Guns from Diablo

Dempsey Clay

A Black Horse Western

ROBERT HALE · LONDON

© Dempsey Clay 2004
First published in Great Britain 2004

ISBN 0 7090 7465 4

Robert Hale Limited
Clerkenwell House
Clerkenwell Green
London EC1R 0HT

Typeset by
Derek Doyle & Associates, Liverpool.
Printed and bound in Great Britain by
Antony Rowe Limited, Wiltshire

CHAPTER 1

FIVE GUNS FROM DIABLO

Standing by the brushwood fence bottle-feeding the sickly lamb, the girl was the first to see the riders.

Her lips moved silently as she counted to five and her dark eyes brightened as they rarely did in this windy season of dust and monotony in the Sheepherder Hills.

They were still far off, coming up along the old Trinidad Trail, which her people had followed here all the way to Utah from New Mexico, when she was just a child.

Few outsiders ever took the trail through the Sheepherders, for there was nothing here but dust and poverty, a thousand black-legged sheep and the dozen *campesino* families who'd made the long journey north-west together only to find themselves as much outsiders here in south-west Utah Territory as they'd been back in New Mexico.

Her name was Josefina. She watched the distant dots slowly grow larger for several minutes, her lush young body relaxed in the flimsy gingham dress her mother claimed was a disgrace, barely listening to her parents wrangling about who'd forgotten to water the vegetable patch last night.

She appeared bored but it was just a pose. The fact that it was five horsemen, not two or ten, was the reason for her interest. Over recent times a particular five riders had fallen into the habit of stopping by here, and as they drew nearer she felt her heart leap when she saw that he was leading them.

Her father cursed behind her. 'Diablo!' he hissed, and spat on the dry earth.

'*Sí*' the girl said dreamily, hugging the lamb to her breast. 'Diablo . . .'

The man glared at her. He was just forty but looked closer to sixty, a gaunt and ravaged sixty with snaggled teeth and burning eyes half-hidden under bushy brows.

'Inside!' he barked. 'And button up your blouse, you look like a whore! Woman, will you speak to your daughter?'

Neither woman moved a muscle and the horsemen loped up to the collapsing gate and reined in.

'Ahh, our *compañeros*!' the sheepman fawned, throwing his arms wide in welcome. '*Por favor*, step down and break bread with us. Woman, girl, food

6

and drink for our splendid young amigos. *Arriba, arriba!*'

But mother and daughter were too busy drinking in the sight of a group of husky, handsome young males, a novel sight in the Sheepherder Hills.

'Much obliged, *señor*,' drawled Gene Taggert, stepping down off his high-shouldered bay. He flicked a glance at the girl, at the way her olive breast-tops caught the light. She waited for his smile before realizing the young Adonis from Diablo was more serious than she'd ever seen him, grim almost. He nodded to her father then indicated Treece's black mustang as its slim-hipped rider jumped to the ground.

'Fetlock strain. I'll trade the horse and twenty dollars for the best mount you can come up with, *paisano*.'

The man gave a gap-toothed grin. He loved to haggle over horses. He started in straight off but Taggert cut him short.

'We're in a hurry, damnit.' He produced a bill-fold and held up a red twenty. 'You've got ten seconds before we go trade with Sanchez instead!'

That was all the 'haggling' took before Bo Treece was stripping his saddle and warbag off the black and began transferring it to a sturdy appaloosa mare which acted up some, wary of outsiders as were all Sheepherder Hills horses, and people.

Taggert was about to remount when the girl suddenly appeared at his side holding an earthen olla and a glass of water. His features softened as he accepted the glass and touched the brim of his sweat-stained hat.

'Much obliged . . . Josefina.'

Her face glowed. '*Por nada*,' she replied gravely. 'It is nothing.'

But, of course, it was more like everything. For this was a young Mexican–American girl who'd spent her life among the small mud villages of the hills where boredom was an everyday fact of life, where sheep bent their heads in placid gray clusters as they fed beyond the hills where little creeks dribbled through the grama grass and the only excitement ever was when someone went loco from boredom and grabbed for a knife or gun.

These so-called gunmen from Diablo were like young gods to her eyes, yet she couldn't help but notice the extra revolvers and saddle rifles they carried, and feel a twinge of fear that they might be riding to danger.

Then he smiled and she worried about nothing but how she looked in that moment, how she wanted to look for him.

They left as quickly as they'd come. But as they clattered away downslope Taggert glanced back once and Josefina waved in response.

'Strumpet!' her father shouted, no sign of his big bogus smile now as he pocketed the twenty spot. 'Do not think I did not see you ogling that desperado. Have I not warned you a thousand times that all from Diablo are gunmen and thieves. And cover yourself. Have you no shame.'

8

She hoped not. And left her blouse exactly as it was as she followed the receding figures with her eyes, hoping he might look back one more time. But he didn't.

He found Big Deke in the Rock Yard leaning on his hammer as he sucked on an illicit smoke out of sight of the bulls.

The moment Yuma's enforcer saw the glint in Kurt Taggert's eye he caught the reek of trouble. It had been building for a long time and it was hardly surprising it should come to a head today, seeing as he'd shoved one of Taggert's bunch of hangers-on through a plate window in the Chow Trough last night.

Deke flicked the butt away and let go of the hammer.

'Y'know, Taggert, I always hated your guts, but I never figured you as dumb.' He shook his rocky block of a head as he spread arms wide and slipped into a fighting crouch. 'But this is dumb, hard-nose, this is as dumb as it gets. One-out, you don't have a prayer against me. You shoulda brung your toadies along.'

Taggert didn't reply, just kept drawing closer until his twenty-stone adversary threw a fist the size of a cantaloupe at his head. Taggert ducked, feinted with his left hand then crashed a fist between Deke's upraised arms to mash his upper teeth against his lips.

Blood sprayed and the heavyweight looked astonished. He roared, ducked, came up impossi-

9

bly fast to connect with a whistling blow to the ear that staggered Taggert and set his head ringing like a dinner gong.

As he slewed to one side the other seized hold of his shirt and ripped it from his body. Taggert caught him with a kick and blocked a swinging forearm to the head that came in retaliation.

In an instant they came brutally together in a vicious toe-to-toe amongst the piles of big rocks waiting to be pounded into little rocks, the bulge of the high wall here cutting them off from the view of the uniformed figures patrolling the parapets above the Rock Yard.

Soon both were bleeding and breathing hard but Taggert's fists kept pistoning into belly, throat and face. Big Deke was throwing fewer blows but each one was weighted like a sledgehammer. Neither spoke, the only sounds the labored breathing, the shuffling of prison-issue boots in gray dust, the ugly thud of knucklebone against flesh.

Suddenly Taggert seemed to lose control. He cursed wildly and swung a haymaker that missed its target by a full foot. Astonished, his opponent chuckled then moved in for the kill, certain of victory now. You always had them when they stopped fighting and began swinging.

Taggert backed up, arms up protectively. He looked wild-eyed and loco yet had seldom been more cool. He was studying his man intently from between upraised fists. Big Deke stood around six feet six with a truly enormous head topped off by a jailhouse haircut that made him look even more the ape than needs be. But most important of all, the giant looked confident – just the way he wanted him.

He slowed his back-pedalling. Deke grinned and charged. Taggert half-turned to one side and raised his left arm to deflect the crunching punch. His right leg shot out and hooked behind Deke's rising left knee. With a fast twist to the right, Taggert heaved back his leg and pushed forward with the total weight of his body behind him. Deke yelled as his legs gave way beneath him. His huge arms swung like windmills as he fell heavily, his bucket-sized skull crashing against a chunk of granite.

The man's eyes rolled in their sockets and before he could move a muscle Taggert's upraised boot smashed down into his face.

He was still kicking the helpless giant when the guards arrived at the run. He knew this meant the Hole, was prepared for it, acted almost offended when he realized they were taking him up upstairs and not down after coming in from the harsh glare of the yard into the main building.

'What's the idea?' he snarled through swollen lips and bloodied teeth. 'Where are we going?' He tried to struggle but the brawl had drained his strength. Next thing he realized he was being frog-marched down a familiar sickly-green corridor of the administration wing, heading for the door marked Warden. 'You've got to be joking,' he panted. 'You don't need James to tell you what that ruckus should fetch. Two weeks in the Hole ...

three tops. Let's get to it then, I can't wait to get started.'

That was sheer bravado. Kurt Taggert was one of the toughest cons in all Yuma, but no man was tougher than the Hole. It was dark, it was cold, it was like you'd died and been buried alive and even the gutsiest of men could eventually find themselves down on their knee praying to be let out or killed, they didn't care much which.

The warden was a middle-aged man of strength, polish and experience who considered Convict 214 calmly.

'Beat Kane to a pulp, I hear, Taggert?' he remarked, sipping coffee from a blue china cup.

His casual gesture saw the sweating bulls leave go of their half-stripped prisoner. Taggert straightened and sleeved his bloodied mouth. He was still breathing heavily. Kane had hurt him plenty before he finished him off.

'What am I doing up here, James?'

The warden leaned back in his comfortable chair. His windows overlooked the main yard and the garden surrounding his private quarters. The sun was shining but no birds sang. No birds ever visited Yuma, not even the buzzards.

'A good question, Taggert. Pithy. Well, I suppose I could say I'm trying to decide whether to have you flogged and tossed in the Hole . . . or if I should release you . . .'

Kurt Taggert's expression didn't alter. They played mind games on a man here as well as the kind played with club and whip.

'So, its going to be like that,' he said. 'Well, whatever jollies you up, Warden.'

The warden set his cup aside and referred to a document on the blotter.

'Hmm . . . Kurt Lucas Taggert, age thirty-six, sentenced to fifteen years for the murder of one Kyle Clanton at Amatina, Utah Territory . . . let's see . . . yes, here it is – that was exactly ten years seven months ago.' He raised his eyes. 'Are these facts and figures accurate, 214?'

'You know they are, you bloodless son of a—'

'Would you not agree that you'd be a highly unlikely felon to be granted a parole, Taggert?'

Parole?

Taggert felt his restraint give way. It was impossible for him to veil his reaction to that word. Nobody joked about something as important as parole to a convict. Nobody ever should, not even a jailhouse boss – the sadistic son of a bitch!

The guards jumped forward as Taggert moved menacingly towards the desk. Yet he managed to restrain himself. He wanted to smash James's smug face into dog-meat but the threat of an even longer stint in solitary held him back. The Hole at Yuma would discourage the Devil from bad-mouthing God.

But he could speak his mind, and was doing that forcefully as the warden leaned back in his chair, folded his soft hands over his comfortable little paunch and waited for him to run out of steam.

Then he said, 'You do me an injustice, 214.' James tapped the document. 'See for yourself. You have been paroled.'

'You're a liar.'

'Read it!'

James's voice cracked with sudden authority. Angry and flushed, Taggert snatched up the paper, noting that it bore the letterhead of the Arizona Department Of Prisons above a subtitle that read: Parole Application No. 1768; Result Thereof.

Next thing he saw was his own name preceding a brief statement to the effect that the parole application lodged on behalf of the 'aforementioned Kurt Lewis Taggert by Gene George Taggert at the sixth sitting of the US Appellate Court, Prescott, on the 6th inst.,' had found that the request had merit and due to 'extenuating circumstances' connected with the prisoner's trial and sentencing, immediate and unconditional parole was to be granted as soon as next of kin were advised.

He read it again, lowered himself slowly to a chair then went over it for a third and final time.

'If this is a joke—'

'I'd never joke about something as serious as this and you know it, man.' James slapped his desk. 'It came as no great surprise to me, of course. I don't need to remind you that there was always something shady and unconvincing about your trial in Utah – as you've never ceased to protest.' The warden shrugged. 'Plainly the powers that be finally got around to reviewing the whole messy affair, and as a result you are free to go as of this minute virtually.'

The toughest con in Yuma felt his legs tremble.

He stared dazedly until finally able to speak.

'When do I leave?'

The warden rose smoothly.

'I won't be sorry to see your back, mister. Matter of fact you've been a nightmare ever since—'

'When?'

'Very well, if that's how you want it. All right, 214, you're eager to be gone, I can't wait for you to go. But before we part company there's one thing I need to know.'

'Oh yeah?'

The warden studied him a moment. Bare-chested, bloodied, scarred and bitter-eyed, Kurt Taggert showed not a vestige of repentance, contrition or a willingness to change. It was not an encouraging sight.

'Those threats you made at your trial. Do you intend attempting to carry them out when you are free?'

'I won't answer that. What I will tell you, Warden, is something you won't believe any more than you did the day they brought me here.' Taggert's eyes were a frozen blue beneath dark brows. 'I didn't kill anybody. I was railroaded by that total bastard Brogan, a lawman I counted a friend. That was my story ten years ago and it's the same today.'

'Mister, every man I face across this desk is innocent – according to his own lights.'

'I ain't every man!'

The interview ended at that point.

When he was alone, James dipped a quill nib in

the inkpot and chewed on the feathered tip. He'd intended writing a letter to the sheriff of Amatina where Taggert had stood trial to inform him that the man had been set free. Then he changed his mind. Why scare them up in Utah if it mightn't be necessary? And if Taggert did go rampaging trouble and landed right back here again, that surely wasn't his problem.

He stepped out on to his balcony to take the evening air. The work gangs were filing into the mess hall, warm lights glowed from his quarters where Mrs James was preparing supper.

He proceeded to the far end of the balcony and gazed out over walls and gun turrets. Twilight was falling and the harsh desert landscape was taking on a kind of strange beauty. There was but one speck of life far out there, a man on a horse provided by the Department of Prisons.

Taggert was tracking north, he saw. But then, that in itself shouldn't suggest anything sinister. Should it?

Sheriff Matt Dunstan finished his shaving and shrugged into a dark sack-coat.

He was an early riser by habit after two decades behind the badge but he rarely rose this early. Intuition told him today the squad of Brogan's Brigadiers visiting from up valley were likely still howling at the moon over at the Palace.

They called themselves militiamen, but at times could act more like wild cowboys at trail's end when Brogan let them run loose.

A gust of cold wind caused him to shiver a little. He buttoned up his dark coat and walked on by the closed doors of the Lucky Deuce and the Valley Realty before turning into Diamond to see lights still burning at the Palace.

His jaws tightened as he quickened his pace.

Many in the valley believed they couldn't do without the volunteer force that made up Brogan's Brigade but Dunstan wasn't one of them. Maybe he couldn't do much about Commander Brogan himself, who was too important, well-connected and too much a hero for a lawman to do anything much, other than accommodate him.

But Brogan and one of his Buffalo Range Ranch scouting parties were two very different things, and the badgeman meant business as he entered the saloon by the rear entrance and headed for the noisy barroom.

'All right, that's enough!' he barked at the four militiamen and their girls as he halted in the doorway. He sniffed at the stink of stale whiskey, perfume and body odour. 'On your way, and lights out. You've got one minute.'

They objected; they always did. A couple looked ready to object until Dunstan put a hard eye on them and they thought better of it.

But one-armed Trask was made of sterner stuff and remained seated as the others were beginning to file out. Matt stroked his moustache.

'Something wrong with your hearing, mister?'

'I'm finishin' my drink, Sheriff.'

'Not in here you're not.' Dunstan jerked a

17

thumb over his shoulder. 'On your way before I arrest you for drunk and disorderly, Trask.'

'That's Officer Trask to you, Dunstan,' the man said, getting up. 'And anyway, we're here on official business for Commander Brogan and—'

'You're drunk, you've outstayed your welcome and you're leaving.'

'OK, OK, no need to get sore.' That was what Trask said, but his look and body language didn't synchronize with his words. The lawman watched him closely as he moved past, with the consequence that the moment the man propped and got ready to swing at him, he was ready.

He could have used a gunbarrel but his fist was handier. The punch only travelled inches but connected with a force that knocked the bigger man to one knee, dazed and hurt.

Trask's men reeled back in and somehow managed to get him out into the yard and into his saddle. The whole party looked sick and sorry in the pale early light; all but 'Officer' Trask.

'Expect to hear from the colonel about this, Dunstan!'

'Get!'

The horses clattered from the yard, trailed after by the weaving figures of the women. Dunstan tugged down the lapels of his coat and examined a skinned knuckle. His moustache stirred. He'd enjoyed that.

Diamond Street was empty end to end when he walked round the front. The glow of the lamps was fading and the dust of the street was a heavy yellow.

The falsefronts stood tall and the iron rooftops gleamed the color of gunmetal.

Nobody was out and about but the Amatina law.

Diamond Street divided Amatina geographically and socially. East, in back of the business houses, were broad streets fronted by fine two- and three-storey houses flanked by heavy trees with servants' quarters in back. West it was some plank-and-batten mixed in with clapboard and the occasional outbreak of tarpaper and adobe brick.

Rich and successful one side, poor and humble about it on the other. Folks knew just where they stood in Amatina where most everybody acknowledged their betters and respected their law.

And the law's name here was Matt Dunstan. He had two deputies to help him out, lived in a converted church and kept casual company with a wealthy woman in her late thirties. That was Matt Dunstan and this was his town and he felt real comfortable with it as he walked to Midge's Diner to get himself one of her steaks before going on to the office.

He was about through with his meal as the sun swung up out of the Sabinosas and Deputy Lomax swung in, clutching his hat and looking edgy.

'Hi, Sheriff,' the young man panted, crossing to his table. 'I was just out exercisin' the jailhouse horses on the south flats when I sighted a bunch of riders cuttin' in towards the stage trail.'

'So?' Matt said lazily. 'Free country, boy. Who are they?'

'Why, that's what I rode back to tell you, Sheriff.

It's Gene Taggert and his bunch from Diablo. And lookin' proddy, seems to me.'

Dunstan was sober as he rose from his table. Around him, the eatery had fallen silent. Bad blood had existed between his town and hardcase Diablo down valley for over the better part of a decade.

The Diablo guns showed up here from time to time, and for dark reasons of his own, the sheriff never relaxed until they had gone again.

The lawman's face had turned hard as he dropped coins on to the table with a clatter. Then he collected his hat and led the deputy toward the doors.

CHAPTER 2

WELCOME HOME

Johnny Ramble was coaxing a tune from his harmonica as weary horses brought them within sight of the big town.

The five rode slowly across the stage trail, then swung down a brown grass slope to follow the winding stream flowing sluggishly between time-worn stones.

Gene Taggert noted how Amatina appeared to have grown even larger and more prosperous-looking since his last visit.

He'd been alone that time, just a tall man on a white horse searching for a little leisure, breathing-space, maybe a pretty woman.

In the end he'd found all three but it hadn't been easy. For he was not only from Diablo, but his name was Taggert. That was two strikes against a man here. Not in every place in Brandaman Valley maybe, but in Amatina for sure.

Diablo's reputation stretched a long way back to the bad old days when it was a haven for outlaws, fast guns, thieves and border-jumpers, and his father was a wanted man. Certainly there were quite a few of that breed still roaming around the Black Rock Hills – he had rep as a hardcase himself.

But in the main Diablo's 'fault' was its taste for independence. The region had been given a bad name in its wild days, and it had stuck despite the efforts to live it down or rise above it by some. Genuine lawmen such as official regional marshal Thompson, or a self-styled one like Commander Brogan, were always threatening to clean up Diablo once and for all, but that had proved easier said than done.

He shrugged as he lighted up.

He knew his hackles were rising already, something he would need to guard against. He held a whole litany of resentments against those who'd hurt his family. The man who wore the sheriff's star was one of them.

'Hey, Gene.'

He turned as Dobbs drew alongside. 'Yeah?'

'We're about there,' replied the blocky young man with an unlit cigar jutting from his teeth. 'You gonna tell us why the hell we're here now?'

'Reckon not.'

Dobbs cussed. 'Why the hell not?'

'I've got good reasons, man.'

'Well,' Dobbs snarled, heeling away, 'make sure you keep 'em to yourself, won't you?'

22

Taggert just grinned. He'd tell them in good time, he mused. He didn't want either his friends or Amatina to know why he was here until he'd had the chance to get a feel for the lie of the land. Simple as that.

Amatina stood upon a long and level broad step ten miles south of the lakes and roughly half-way down the eighty-mile length of the valley which stretched from Delta Fork in the north to the Arizona border in the south.

Treece, Ramble, Dobbs and Carlaw fell silent as they followed Taggert up onto the stage road again and dusted past the first houses.

They were expected. They could tell this by the number of people on the street, the way a bunch of kids scuttled from sight over by the feed-and-grain barn.

Taggert glanced down. He wore twin Colts in cutaway holsters with a saddle rifle under his right knee. His friends were similarly well armed. He'd warned there could be trouble here before they set out. He sure as hell wasn't looking to raise any dust, just wanted to be ready in case.

He was relaxing some by the time they reached Coyote Street.

Up ahead stood the Palace, biggest and best saloon-hotel in the valley. Opposite he saw a clerk from Goodfellow's store pause to stare, then resume his sweeping with a burst of nervous energy. A Conestoga with a broken axle stood in the wagon yard and a man holding a wrench stared out at them in surprise, then suddenly grinned and touched hatbrim.

Gene eased his seat in the saddle.

The town appeared normal, he decided. It was he who was edgy, and there was one sure cure for that. Jerking on his left rein he led the way down the alley to the Champion livery stables. From there they walked back to the Palace.

'Nice sherry, Clara.'

'Thank you, Matthew. Another?'

'Maybe not.'

'Duty?'

'Something like that, I guess.'

Clara Briet eyed her guest questioningly as they stepped through the french doors from the elegant parlor onto the paved balcony overlooking the gardens where an old man under a big straw hat was weeding the roses.

The widow Briet had the finest garden in Amatina. It had become her passion since losing her wealthy merchant husband in a boating accident. As they stood at the railing she studied the sheriff curiously.

'I must say I'm surprised you're still here this late, Matthew,' she remarked. Then added hastily, 'Not that I mind, of course, the opposite rather.'

He felt a little guilty when she spoke that way. For there was no romance, even though she might wish it were otherwise. He was alone, had been ever since the turbulent and tragic days of a decade ago; she was a handsome woman left on her own. They got along well, he liked coming

24

here, or the occasional outing together. But that was it.

'Why, where do you think I should be, Clara?'

'Well, naturally I thought . . . I mean . . . under the circumstances . . .'

'You mean the Diablo bunch?'

'Well, everyone's talking about them. And everyone knows how that Taggert boy hates you, Matthew. As for those renegade friends of his, if he told them to jump under a train I'm sure they would do it. Aren't you at least uneasy?'

Of course he was. But then, uneasiness was an everyday reality when you were responsible for law and order in a region this size.

'There are two ways of dealing with trouble, Clara. You can tackle it head-on the moment it appears, or you can sit back and do nothing, and who knows, it might just go away.'

'Would you care to stay for supper?'

'Tempting, Clara. But I reckon this trouble – if that's what it is – hasn't gone away just yet. Much obliged for a very pleasant evening.'

The sheriff returned to the main street at the same steady pace, an easy-moving man who radiated calm and control regardless of whatever might be going on inside.

And behind his lawman's façade, he was edgy as hell over the arrival of the gun-packing Diablo five.

For Gene Taggert hated him and had done ever since the trial that had seen his older brother draw fifteen years for the murder of Kyle Clanton right here at the courthouse. A raging Kurt Taggert had vowed to square accounts with Dunstan that day, and every time they'd met since he'd seen the same hate glitter in the younger brother's stare.

Gene was little more than a gangly kid when they took his brother off to Yuma. He was no kid now. He'd grown bigger than Kurt and had a reputation as a quiet man it didn't pay to cross. Just last year, some border jumper showed up in Diablo, got into a scrape with Gene Taggert and wound up on a slab.

Yet despite incidents like that Diablo still expected the valley to believe they were innocent victims of gossip down there.

Tell him another!

He hit Diamond and swung right. The Palace stood half a block away. His shadow fell on the darkened porch of an office with an AMATINA FOR COUNTY SEAT placard in the window.

The movement campaigning for Amatina to become the county capital was led with unrelenting vigor by Commander Brogan and had made front page news in the *Express* all this week. Tomorrow the paper would likely carry a different lead. Editors loved it whenever Diablo grabbed the headlines.

The Palace was filled with noise and rough laughter as he shouldered through the doors and drinkers made way respectfully as he headed for the long mahogany bar. By the time he reached the bar he'd spotted the big bronzed man drinking beer with Lottie Hanrahan at the far end of the bar.

'What'll it be, Sheriff?'

'My usual, Lon. And whatever the young folks are drinking yonder.'

The noise level dropped sharply at that. But when the drinks had been delivered the sheriff hoisted his rye and raised it in a toast.

'Welcome to Amatina again, Mr Taggert. And your good health, Lottie.'

The girl smiled. Taggert didn't. He looked peeved, was peeved. But he was no firebrand like his brother. He had a self-control that was hard to shake.

So he just nodded, touched his new glass with the one he was drinking from, sipped.

Reassured, Matt carried the drink the length of the bar to join them on their high bar stools.

'How're things down south, Gene?'

'OK. Up here?'

'Quiet. Apart from all the hooraw about the county seat, that is.' Matt glanced round. 'Your friends desert you?' he grinned.

'Guess Lottie scared them off with her singing.'

'Speaking of which,' the girl said nervously, sliding to ground, 'I've a number coming up . . .'

She hurried off. Matt felt the weight of blue eyes on him. 'So, what's on your mind, Dunstan?'

Matt studied his glass. 'Just hoping we don't have any trouble while you boys are here, son. You know me. I like to keep my town—'

'Sure, I know you, mister. I know you from way back.'

The sheriff sighed. For a minute there he'd

hoped things might have changed. He saw he was wrong. It was still trial day ten years back for this man of the south. Gene Taggert had forgotten nothing.

'Very well,' he said firmly. 'Let's understand one another. You boys are welcome to stay here just as long as you like, providing you don't make trouble. If you do I'll come down on you hard. Understood?'

'I reckon I always understood you.' Taggert's eyes were glittering from something he carried inside.

'Sorry it has to be this way.' Matt turned to go, paused. 'I want an answer to one question. Why are you here?'

'Is that a trick question, lawman? You know, the kind a man like might ask all innocent, then by the time you get to court, twist it round so that you don't recognize what you said anymore – and you could find yourself branded guilty of something you didn't do. Like what happened to Kurt.'

The sheriff tossed his drink down and headed for the batwings, tall in the doorway before he disappeared. Taggert stared at the faces surrounding him until every eye dropped. He reached for his drink with a steady hand. Lottie was just beginning her number in a high, untrained soprano.

CHAPTER 3

THE COMMON ENEMY

Gene Taggert heard the first rooster crow of the morning two days later. He sat up on his bed at Buck's Trailhouse, still fully dressed and just as wide awake at whatever sparrow-chirp time it might be now as he'd been way back at midnight.

The trailhouse was silent all about him. He'd heard the others returning to their rooms at what seemed like hours ago to him now. He'd had his lamp turned out so they wouldn't come barging in, half-cut and eager to recount what a great night they'd had.

He grimaced.

He knew he was poor company these days.

But he had his reasons and they were major ones.

Moving to the window, he gazed out. It was rain-ing some and dawn was still a little way off.

'The hell with it!' he said aloud, buckled on his twin Colts, jammed his hat on the back of his head and went out front through the dimly lit lobby. Might as well walk as waste time pretending he might drop off eventually.

Some time later he realized that his unplanned route had brought him to the courthouse. He'd avoided the building up until now because of the bad memories. They began crowding in again immediately and it all came back, the pain, the shock, his brother's hoarse voice: *Kid, I'm innocent. They know it . . . Dunstan knows it . . . that lousy fake of a judge damnwell knows it. And Brogan was behind it, every step of the way, pulling strings, poisoning them against me. He hated the old man and he hates me . . . us! But I'll get square if it takes fifty years. . . .*

He was just a kid when it all happened, still weeks shy of his fourteenth birthday; his father already long dead and his only brother up in Amatina facing a killing charge.

Even that long ago the Taggert brothers had already secured their own piece of land, the T-2 – Taggers Two – and were more involved in ranching, horse-trading and building up the place as a working spread rather than raising hell.

He was out herding steers alone along Ripple Creek the day that he heard the evil news about Kurt. By the time he reached Amatina it was all over. They'd found Kurt guilty of killing Kyle Clanton mainly, or so it seemed, due to the fact that the two had battered each other in a fierce brawl at the Medusa saloon earlier the same day.

Brogan and his 'Brigade' were in town still celebrating Kurt's conviction when Gene rode in. Throughout the days of the trial Brogan had conducted a sustained vilification programme against the 'Diablo scum gunmen', which had patently affected the outcome.

Yet Kurt's rage was directed mainly against his former friend, Matt Dunstan. He insisted to Gene that although the lawman knew him to be innocent he'd finally buckled under the sustained pressure of Brogan's campaign and a 'personal matter' to see him convicted.

Gene had only discovered later that Tessa McNair had finally made a choice between her two admirers, and had chosen Kurt.

He was still swearing to get square with everyone who'd done him wrong as they hauled him off to Yuma.

Gene had visited his brother on several occasions, but not for a long time now. He'd grown to manhood over those long years and somehow Kurt seemed to expect him to do something about his situation.

What could he do?

So eventually he quit the cross-country Arizona journeys altogether, seeing no point in visiting the pen just to listen to his brother chronicle all his hatreds and resentments.

Instead, Gene had concentrated on the ranch, constantly building it up, making improvements and largely staying out of trouble in order that big brother would have something solid to come back to when they let him out.

Something more than vengeance with a gun.

A gust of cold rain blew in on him under the overhang and jolted him back to the present. He stared up at the courthouse's great doors, then moved back down to the plankwalk beneath a dark sky that had lost its moon.

Maybe, he'd been wrong about what Kurt might do, he mused optimistically, as he set off on his way again. About what he might do when he got free – that was.

The sole reason he'd strapped on his shooters and headed north after being notified of his brother's parole was the fear that Kurt would head here intent upon carrying out his old threats.

But there was still no sign of him, so why shouldn't a man start hoping?

Maybe he'd gone directly back home to Diablo? Maybe he'd learned his lesson the hard way and come to realize just how lucky he was to have those long years sliced off his time. Maybe even realized he was still young enough to grab himself a whole new life with both hands?

He'd be the happiest man in Utah if that was so.

A dim light caught his eyes as he passed the bank. Next door, Midge Riddle was already open for business even though it was barely light. Half-grinning now, he sloshed through the puddles and went in to grab a mug of good joe and a big slice of pie. He nodded amiably to the half-awake customers before paying his check and leaving.

He was half-way across Diamond when he paused to make way for the rider who emerged suddenly out of the winding gray sheets of mizzling rain.

The horseman was hunched under a gleaming yellow slicker, the trail-stained horse plainly footsore. He looked up. The figure in the saddle was tall and lean with a corncob pipe jutting from his teeth. He inhaled vigorously and by the bowl's cherry-red glow Gene caught the outline of a hawkish profile, taut cheekbones and hard jawline.

He felt his heart flip.

'Kurt?'

The horse jerked to a halt as the rider hipped around in his saddle, staring intently. Then:

'Well I'll be damned. What in the Sam Hill are you doin' here, kid brother?'

The ragged kid walking the country trail three days later looked over his shoulder and let out a yell.

'Lookit, Mom, riders!'

The shabbily dressed woman took one look at the onrushing line of horsemen approaching swiftly from behind. She quickly seized the child by the arm and hauled him off the shoulder of the road into the grassy ditch.

The horsemen came storming by with scarcely a glance, jaws set and eyes on the trail ahead, all dressed in a quasi-military style with big hats and wide pouch-belts which flapped up and down to the rhythm of their horses.

Only the leader wore a tunic of deep royal blue with golden epaulets, a wide-brimmed hat turned up at one side and ornamented with an ostrich feather. He was tall and bearded with burning eyes. A saber swung from the broad belt buckled around his hips. Leaning forward in his big double-girthed Texas-Spanish saddle, his gaze seemed fixed on the horizon, locked there as the clouds of hoof-lifted dust they'd raised engulfed the woman and the boy and left them coughing in their wake.

'Who were they, Mama?'

The woman's face showed pale with unease, yet she tried to sound confident and reassuring as they clambered out of the ditch.

'That's the Commander and some of his men on his way to something important, I'm sure, Billy. They look out for poor folks like us, keep us safe.'

'Safe from what?'

'Why, whatever there is, I suppose. There's always something for honest folks to be fearful of, I guess.'

Gene found his brother drinking alone at the Drumhead saloon. Kurt scowled but Gene's face was blank. They'd barely spoken since their fierce argument on meeting. An angry Kurt had accused Gene of believing he'd ridden directly from Yuma to Amatina planning to square accounts with Dunstan and everybody else involved in his conviction.

An equally intense Gene had insisted he'd come

north praying Kurt wouldn't show. Yet the fact that Kurt had arrived convinced him he had vengeance on his mind, which in turn could be interpreted as proof that maybe he really was the killer as the law had branded him all those years ago.

After the dust of that first clash had cleared Gene had pleaded with his brother to return to Diablo. Kurt flatly refused. They'd avoided each other ever since. Now Gene arrived with an olive branch.

'We're having a drink over at the Palace. The boys'd like to see you. You can't hold it against them just for riding up with me. I didn't tell them what I was fearful of in case I was wrong.'

'So, you admit you were wrong?'

'Like hell I do.'

'Then what's keeping you?'

'I'll go when I want, if I want.'

Kurt Taggert paled. When he'd gone to prison his brother had been a stripling boy he could whup one-handed. But he'd realized in their first minute together just how greatly Gene had changed. Not only was he a bigger man than himself but there was a balance and sureness about him now that a man couldn't overlook.

He waved a careless hand. 'Just go, kid, leave me be.'

'Not until I've heard something from you.'

'What, damn you?'

'If you didn't come to back to square accounts with Matt Dunstan about the trial and the woman—'

35

'Never mind the woman. And she has a name. Tessa McNair—'

'Then why did you come back here?' Gene finished stubbornly. 'Answer me that.'

For a long moment it seemed the other wasn't going to reply. Then, taking a swig of his drink and studying his bronzed image in the bar mirror, Kurt said simply:

'Why, to clear my name of course.'

'You don't know how much I want to believe that, Kurt.'

'You can believe it. Now if there's nothing else. . . ?'

'OK, I'm going, I'm going.' Gene turned for the doors, paused. 'Maybe later?'

'Maybe. Take it easy.'

'You too.'

White Howlett whistled to keep up his spirits as his horse carried him back towards the town. He was a rugged man with a black beard, hunked heavily in the shoulders with meat. His cheeks were flushed and he swayed just a little in the saddle as he rode up from the river having drunk a tad too much at his one-man spread out along the Comstock Road.

He'd run out of whiskey at breakfast, wasn't sure if it was his need for just a little more, or defiance, that was taking him to town. Maybe a bit of both.

It was quiet when he entered the beat-up old Melodian, just the barkeep polishing glasses, a tired-face girl playing solitaire and no more than a dozen early drinkers.

He tried to ignore the sudden silence and wary looks that greeted him as he bought himself a treble and toted it to a corner table. He swaggered a little as he walked. He was big and mean and packed a Colt. With a reputation as a brawler, and no stranger to Sheriff Dunstan's cells, Howlett was a good man to avoid, drunk or sober, especially when in the mood he was in today.

He slugged down half his drink and commenced fashioning a quirley with big blunt fingers. Conversations were starting up again but he detected an undertone of whispering here and there. It didn't take much imagination to guess what they were saying.

'He looks scared, and got a right to be, I reckon.'

Or, 'Mebbe he should've stayed gone longer'n a couple of days, don't you reckon? I mean, we ain't forgot the part he played in Taggert's trial, and you can bet money Taggert ain't neither.'

Howlett lighted his smoke and drew deeply as he cut his eyes to the batwings. The liquor warmed his belly and he was feeling defiant again. What did he have to be scared about anyway? Just because he'd given testimony against Kurt Taggert at his trial, or that now Taggert had come back years ahead of his sentence time, didn't mean he was at any kind of risk, did it? This was a law-abiding town these days. Dunstan kept it that way.

Customers drifted in and out during the following half-hour. Howlett got up and bought a second drink and was just resuming his seat when a clatter of bootheels on the porch outside preceded the sound of hands slamming against the tops of swinging doors and four men packing guns came striding in, headed boisterously for the bar, then propped.

They stared at the big man drinking alone.

It was simple chance that had brought Treece, Carlaw, Dobbs and Ramble to the Melodian. They'd been in high spirits since Kurt Taggert's return had turned Amatina on its ear, for they anticipated trouble and had never been averse to a little excitement.

Although they'd seen little of either brother over the past forty-eight hours the T-2 bunch was aware of the tensions between Gene and Kurt and the jittery reaction of the town, but so far didn't know where it all might lead. So they did what they did best, spread themselves around, sparked the girls, did some light gambling and drinking – and waited.

They'd almost forgotten White Howlett over the years but remembered him quickly the moment they sighted him, who he was and what he'd done. Howlett was one of those Kurt had threatened from the dock the day they hauled him away to Arizona.

'Thought they said he'd quit town,' Ramble drawled after a silence. 'Mebbe he should've . . .'

'Sonuva,' grunted Dobbs. But then he shrugged. 'But what the hell. He's nothin' to us. Besides, remember Gene's warnin'.'

Heads nodded. They remembered good. Gene

had made it crystal clear they were to keep their noses clean while he settled things down with Kurt. It always made good sense to do whatever Gene said when he got that certain hard blue glint in his eye.

Shrugging, they continued on to the bar, ordered beers, started yarning amongst themselves. But that wasn't what it looked like to the big man across the room. Howlett should have been trying to sober up, not putting more of the hard stuff away the way he was. The man was scared, angry, jittery and full of whiskey-fuelled pride as he watched the Diablo party. He was imagining them gearing up to make a move against him, against the Taggerts' enemy.

His gaze moved over the room. He realized the other drinkers had all gone quiet again, expectant.

Maybe they figured he might quit and run.

The hell he would!

He rose suddenly, knocking over his chair. The sharp clatter brought the Diablo party whirling about, and Howlett's liquor-fogged vision interpreted this sudden movement as threatening.

'Sons of bitches!' he shouted furiously, and fumbled for his gun handle.

'No, Johnny!' a white-faced Bo Treece shouted as the slender figure at his side went into his draw. 'The big mucker's just drunk!'

Too late. Ramble caught the flash of a naked sixgun and saw the menacing face behind it. That was enough. He squeezed trigger and the crash of his .44 rocked the barroom and sent a billowing, surging gush of gunsmoke towards Howlett as something slammed him backwards into the wall, his unfired gun spinning the air and clattering to the floor.

Grimacing, white with shock, Howlett appeared sober in a moment as he clutched his right shoulder. Blood squeezed through his fingers. He lifted his head to stare round the room and tears filled his red-rimmed eyes.

'Damned idjut!' Johnny Ramble said disgustedly, housing his cutter. 'What'd he go and do that for?'

'Mebbe the sheriff can figure that out,' said a sober-faced Carlaw. 'Guess somebody better go fetch him, huh?'

The doctor closed his worn black bag with a snap.

'He'll be OK now. Just a flesh wound.' He looked around the law office which was beginning to appear crowded. 'Good shooting. Or lucky.'

'Good shootin',' insisted Dobbs. 'Damn good, truth to tell. The bum was fixin' to ventilate us for no good reason—'

'It's OK, boys.' Gene stood tall in the archway leading to the cells, thumbs hooked in shell belt. 'I reckon the sheriff's got the story straight by this. Ain't that so, Dunstan?'

'That's Sheriff Dunstan,' Matt said from his desk chair.

'Whatever.' Gene's jaw was tight.

'Whatever doesn't do it,' Dunstan said flatly, his lined face impassive. 'What's my name, Taggert?'

40

Everyone looked uneasily at Gene with the exception of Howlett, slumped in a chair nursing his slinged arm. The atmosphere was tense in the aftermath of the gunplay. Dunstan's two deputies stood behind his chair staring across at Taggert. Gene flicked his eyes at his pards momentarily, then let a held breath go. He was mad about what had happened, not at Dunstan. He had troubles enough without tangling with the law.

'Sheriff Dunstan,' he said, and everybody relaxed a little. 'And I've got a first name.'

'Sure you have, Gene.' Matt Dunstan's manner was easy in an instant. He'd made his point and was ready to get on with the matter in hand. Having already formed a clear picture of what had taken place at the saloon, he reckoned he understood both what had happened, and why. He supposed he could make a case of it if he wanted, but didn't see the point. Howlett had been both scared and drunk, he'd pulled iron and had been creased for his trouble.

The sheriff of Amatina had larger matters on his mind at the moment.

White Howlett, scarcely recognizable as the proddy, red-faced drunk who'd taken his troubles to the Melodian mid-morning, couldn't believe his luck when Dunstan sent him packing without recording a charge. He was advised to get back to his one-man outfit on the Comstock Road and stay there, advice the hardcase surprisingly followed. It enabled him to survive the uncertain days ahead when men were destined to die.

The judge, the same judge who'd passed sentence upon Kurt Taggert at his trial, cursed a little and scratched irritably at his straggly beard as Howlett left. He'd have thrown the book at the man if Matt had wanted, but as always at times like this it was the sheriff who called the shots and ran the show. It was simply the way things were.

When Dunstan had dismissed the witnesses from the Melodian and sent his deputies off on patrol, he was left alone with the Diablo five, a half-pannikin of cold coffee and an opportunity he hadn't had since the Diablos' arrival in his town. Namely, to get a few things straight and clear the air.

'You were informed ahead of time that Kurt had been paroled,' he said to Gene. It wasn't a question but a statement.

'Yeah.'

'And so you figured he'd come here first?'

'Reckoned he might.'

'Naturally you came to join him and just happened to bring four guns with you?'

'Pards, not guns.'

'Why?'

At this Treece, Carlaw, Dobbs and Ramble all leaned forward intently. They didn't know why Gene had brought them north either. They had hunches, but didn't know.

'In case of trouble.' Gene's tone was flat, guarded.

Dunstan's stare drilled at him. 'What kind of trouble, mister?'

42

'Who knows?'

Dunstan was testy as he rose and came round his desk. He stood before Gene in the archway. The men were of a height but Taggert exuded strapping power while the lawman was lean and spare.

'It couldn't just be,' Dunstan said with slow deliberation, 'that you reckoned your brother might come here to square accounts like he threatened at his trial, could it? And that you figured that you and these gunslick friends of yours might back his play?'

A look of puzzlement crossed Gene's face.

'Is that what you think? You couldn't be further off-target, mister.'

'Don't lie to me, boy.'

'I'm not lying, and I'm no boy.'

A shadow fell through the jailhouse doorway and Kurt Taggert stood there, arms hanging loose at his sides, hat thrust back from his forehead.

'He's right on both counts, Sheriff,' he stated easily, coming in. He nodded all round then removed his hat and tossed it carelessly onto the desk. He ran fingers through an unruly thatch, a muscular, hungry-looking man burned dark by the south-western sun, scarred, calloused and as durable-looking as cured rawhide. He winked at Ramble. 'So, who'd you shoot, kid?'

'It wasn't anything,' Gene said tersely. 'Right, Sheriff?'

'A minor incident. But I still want to know why you came up to Amatina right at this time.'

43

'You and us both,' said Dobbs. 'How about it, Gene?'

Gene sighed. There seemed no point in holding back now, so he told them. It was the truth. He'd simply feared Kurt might attempt something he'd regret and he'd be here to stop him.

The sheriff digested what he'd heard, then broke the silence.

'I see,' he murmured, flicking his coat tails back and thrusting both hands into his pants pockets. He cocked an eyebrow at the young guns. 'Maybe you men would like to wait outside while we discuss a few matters?'

'Heck, do we have to?' Eli Carlaw objected. 'This is just gettin' interestin'.'

'Better do like the man says.' Gene stared from one to the other until they eventually shrugged, reached for their tobacco and walked out.

Dunstan eyed Kurt Taggert levelly. 'Let's get right down to cases. Do you still believe I rail-roaded you?'

'Not think,' Kurt corrected, eyes ice-blue, cold as freezing-point. 'Know.'

Fierce argument erupted immediately as Gene made his way round the desk and lowered himself into the sheriff's chair. Accusation and counter accusation filled the air as he lifted boots on to the desk top and leisurely crossed one leg over the other. He was half-listening to the wrangling while allowing his mind to drift back to when it had all happened.

The two had been friends then, Kurt and

Dunstan; the peace officer of Amatina and the hardcase from Diablo. But reputations could be deceptive. Dunstan, for example, wasn't quite as rigid as he sometimes appeared. And it was a fact of Diablo life that Kurt Taggert, like Gene himself, had inherited a wild reputation from their outlaw father which they carried to this day without ever having been involved in anything really serious enough to warrant it. Diablo was an independent pocket of hard riders and hardcases, but old Charlie Taggert would have been ashamed of the way they failed to live up to his example.

Kurt and Dunstan had been friends and maybe still would be but for Tessa McNair.

To this day Gene didn't know even half the story of that turbulent triangle which had held Amatina enthralled back when. But he had always believed that it had been the case of a woman coming between good friends that had first set in motion the train of events which had eventually carried his brother to a murder trial, conviction and, at the last, off to the living hell of Yuma.

He opened a drawer and took out one of Dunstan's cigars. The two were still at it but calmer and quieter now, although the bitterness on Kurt's part and the resentment on Dunstan's seemed strong as ever.

But nothing was being decided and might well never be, so he reckoned. Seemed to him the gap separating them was just too wide; too much dirty water had gone beneath the bridge.

Eventually he grew tired of it. He set the freshly

45

lighted stogie between his teeth, lowered his boots and was about to rise when he heard it.

From somewhere up along Diamond Street came the sudden rumble of hoofbeats approaching through the central block at a gait far too fast for safety. Someone yelled, another man hooted and through the barred windows he glimpsed people jumping up onto the walks for safety and gesticulating excitedly at something beyond his view.

Dunstan and Kurt quit arguing The sheriff beat Gene through the door, shading his eyes with one hand as the phalanx of incoming horsemen crossed Coyote and then began to slow as they reached Goodfellow's store on the central block. Bright harness, guns and a lofty flag glinted in the dusty light as the sheriff of Amatina breathed a soft curse.

'The goddamn militia! That's all we need!'

The brothers from Diablo traded tight glances as a towering bearded figure in a gaudy uniform reined in his lathered mount in front of the council chambers building and raised a gauntleted hand to bring his dozen-strong party of riders behind to a halt.

In that moment, in the face of possible trouble, the brothers from Diablo were at last back on the old footing together, strong and sure of one another. For this, more than any other, was the common enemy.

CHAPTER 4

TESSA

An errant breeze stirred the commander's wispy beard. He smoothed it with a gloved hand as he gazed somberly and thoughtfully above the heads of the crowd he had immediately attracted, rocking gently to and fro in his big black boots.

They waited for him to continue. One moment he'd been in full cry, damning the common enemies of Diablo, drouth, outlawry in general, overweening piety and, of course, Delta Fork, the rival town at the north of the valley which had the gall to be competing with Amatina to secure the official nomination as county seat. He'd even taken time to make it known that the Brigade was hot on the heels of the outlaw Wild Bob Killane – 'the Diablo dastard' as he incorrectly labelled him – which brought cheers all around. But now, not a word.

The mob began to fidget. The commander of

Brogan's Brigade had a worsening reputation for eccentricity. His political enemies labelled him as crazy and a potential danger to the very law and order he professed to champion. None could deny he was manifesting increasingly extreme and disturbing habits, yet even his many enemies found it hard to contest the fact that he'd always seemed to have the best interests of the valley at heart.

For Commander Brogan went a long way back here. A former rider with Rangle's Raiders in the War, he'd come to the valley with a high reputation which he quickly exploited to become a landowner, political force, a fierce hater of Indians, lawbreakers and anyone who opposed him in any of his many fields of endeavor. But his chief claim to fame was as a vigilante leader.

Brogan's Brigade had started off as a small band of private militia which, in a primitive region as the valley was in those days, soon built up a reputation for Indian fighting and stringing up cow-thieves.

The law had been uneasy about all this at first, but after a time concluded that the commander's excesses were outweighed by his zealous successes against all his perceived enemies, and for years the courts, the army and the territorial government in Salt Lake City had all virtually come to condone his largely lawful role as lawbringer and enforcer, turning a blind eye to his paramilitary operations providing he didn't go too far.

Diablo was regarded by both the valley and Brogan himself as his one failure. There'd been personal enmity between him and old Charlie Taggert, and over the years Brogan had made several concerted – and failed – attempts to clean out that 'outlaw's nest.'

The trial and conviction of Kurt Taggert had seen Brogan seem almost to lose interest in Diablo as he pursued far more important goals, in particular his obsession with seeing Amatina made county capital.

Taggert's release seemed to have jolted the commander ten years back in time and only his close henchmen understood the fury and outrage that had brought them here today.

Brogan had many admirers here but just as many enemies. But even his enemies could not deny that as a speaker the commander had few equals.

Plainly he was about to continue his address now as he climbed to a high position on the chamber steps, and a buzz of excitement swept the throng. Who would the old outlaw hunter be tearing verbal strips off next, they speculated, although most believed they could guess.

Brogan cleared his throat and lowered his gaze to the mob. It seemed to take him a long time to focus.

'He's coming!' he declared forcefully.

Glances were exchanged. People frowned. What was he talking about? He'd just taken sideswipes at Delta Fork, namy-pamby lawmakers – a favorite target, and 'filthy, disease-ridden pockets of outlawry and perpetuation of the criminal species'

– which meant Diablo, or so everybody guessed. Now he was off on another tangent altogether. Who was coming?

'None other than the commissioner of counties for all Utah Territory!' he bellowed triumphantly, ramming a gloved fist overhead. 'Those fustian, self-seeking demagogues of the Wasatches have finally agreed to leave their beloved Salt Lake City and their evil and unnatural obsessions with money, power and polygamy to venture southward and see for themselves how magnificently we have developed our mighty valley and how richly this wonderful town of yours has earned the right to be bestowed with the crown of county capital! I'm reliably informed that the commissioner and his party could be here within the month to inspect the region at first hand and assess Amatina's qualifications to receive the town patent!'

They cheered him to the echo. Commander Brogan knew how to whip up a crowd. He was a strange kind of hero in the valley, having mixed his early rough-riding activities with his capacity as a political organizer with successful ranching, business investment, lobbying the government and eventually his most enduring and famous role as chief of of his own private militia.

The militia caught on fast in a developing region and before too long it became the comfortable habit of the valley to expect Brogan's Brigade to show up whenever there was a lawless outbreak or when the official law forces proved incompetent – as so determined by Commander Oliver Brogan.

He made a theatrical figure today as he paced to and fro with members of his militia jumping forwards to clear the way for him when necessary, his personal gunmen and bodyguards in close attendance.

Trask's badge of honor was his empty left shirt-sleeve. The limb had been amputated several years earlier following the brigade's last failed and bloody attempt to clean up the commander's personal obsession, the town, the region and the way of rebellious life known as Diablo.

Diablo represented Brogan's single, significant failure as boss of his own private army.

So it was that nobody was surprised when he suddenly switched topics from the general to the specific following the quiet but significant arrival at the chambers building of the Diablo bunch.

Suddenly he was only concerned with them – forget about town patents, the vagaries of the parole system and the notorious hellion whose pursuit had brought him here, Wild Bob Killane.

The commander showed he was right up to date on the most recent developments involving his detested enemy and those involved with them, either friendly or hostile.

'It grieves me deeply, my fellow citizens and visionaries of the valley, to note that since my last visit a foul and unrepentant murderer has been granted a parole and has returned here to spread his pernicious influence once again.'

He propped and raised a finger high.

'And that now his whole murderous bunch of

backshooters and Diablo street-sweepings should have returned to join him and haunt us and parade their infamous and vicious ways before all you fine and decent people ... who deserve so much better!'

All eyes were on the Taggert bunch now. But if they anticipated angry reaction they were to be disappointed. All six, Kurt, Gene and the others could display impressive poker faces when they chose, and did so now.

This seemed to anger Brogan who feigned unawareness of the group leaning casually against the pillars at the southern end of the marble gallery as he continued to pace to and fro, yet each time he turned back their way his steps led him a little closer.

The party stood their ground. This was a free country.

'Ah yes, men and women of Amatina, the struggle is surely unending. Today, by coincidence it may seem, is my fourth day in pursuit of a man who first came to notoriety as henchman and disciple of a piece of Diablo filth named Charlie Taggert, who happily left us for Hades many years ago but not, regrettably, before begetting two of his evil progeny among us who are actually polluting our sweet pure air here today. How outrageous! But how fortunate we stopped by!'

Brogan reached the far limit of his pacing, paused a moment to finger-comb his whiskers then started back towards the bunch.

This time Gene Taggert sensed the ranting

figure would come all the way and attempt to bluster them off the gallery, the kind of arrogant theatrical ploy that would appeal to this man.

He glanced at his pards. They nodded. They were solid. He flicked a glance across at his brother and felt a stir of unease. He was ready to stand fast against Brogan himself but didn't want Kurt caught up in anything serious. He wasn't convinced that a combined enemy comprising the law, Brogan and the system might not be capable of putting Kurt back behind bars if given half an excuse.

Kurt's expression remained blank. A man could rarely tell what he was thinking these days. But at least Gene knew exactly what he was thinking. He wasn't moving.

The tall figure kept talking and coming. Three militiamen, burly and officious, mounted the gallery ahead of him and motioned several citizens off the steps. They approached the bunch, bootheels cracking hard.

'Clear the way, clear the way. What's the matter? You men deaf?'

Dobbs said distinctly, 'We hear real good. I just been listenin' to an outhouse door bangin' in the wind.'

The militiamen paused, shocked. The commander was coming up behind. He suddenly broke off his speech, realizing he'd been insulted. Coloring hectically, he raised his heavy riding-crop high and shouldered his men roughly aside to lunge directly at Gene, eyes blazing with outrage.

'Offal! Outlaw offal and a blight upon all of us. By God and by glory, their house is the gateway to hell going down to the chambers of death! Feel the wrath of your betters, renegade trash!'

He swung wildly, viciously. Without even moving his feet, Gene swayed back a little. The blow missed and Brogan followed it, falling forward to tumble down the broad marble steps, roaring as he fell, then suddenly silent as he struck.

For a moment the street was hushed. Then brigadiers rushed forward to haul the tall man to his feet. The rest menaced the troublemakers, brandishing batons and confident in their strength of numbers with Trask leading them, hand on gunbutt.

A uniformed figure jolted Kurt with his shoulder. Always volatile, Kurt lashed out with a vicious punch to the side of the face that knocked the militiaman bowlegged, reeling away sideways before going down in a heap, spitting crimson.

Nobody saw where the sheriff came from. One moment there was space between the Diablos and the militia, the next Matt Dunstan was there, tall and calm.

'That will do it!' he said in a voice that carried. 'What just happened was nothing and will remain nothing.' He gestured in the hush. 'The commander doesn't look well. Get him along to the doctor immediately. That other man also.'

He moved to the edge of the gallery, raising his voice.

'That's all for today, ladies and gents. The

commander thanks you for coming and so do I.'
He turned to bend a hard stare on the hesitant
militiamen. 'Well, what are you waiting for?'

For a moment it seemed Trask might defy him,
but after a long taut moment the man eased his
single hand off his gunbutt and stepped back,
likely figuring that one gunfighter against six was
not the sort of odds a man chanced if he wanted to
see his grandkids.

Turning his head, the commander's man cursed
and snapped an order. Immediately the militiamen backed up, then jumped down the steps and
hurried to Brogan's assistance. He wasn't hurt but
his demeanor was alarming as they led him away.
Empty-eyed and shambling, he didn't seem to
understand what had happened, or even where he
was. He'd gone from wild-eyed demagogue to
stumbling old man in the space of a minute.

'Much obliged, Sheriff.'

Dunstan turned to Gene, who'd spoken.

'I was just doing my job,' he replied. 'That was
fairly provocative, what you did.'

Gene folded muscular arms.

'Depends on your point of view, I guess. We had
more right to stay put than that old glory-hunter
had to move us on. It's called equality.'

Matt grimaced. 'Seems you've turned into a
bush lawyer since you were here last, Taggert.'

'That's Gene or Mr Taggert to you. Remember
. . . Sheriff Dunstan? But who can say? Maybe some
good lawyers, bush or otherwise, is what's needed
hereabouts. I mean, the law isn't always fair or seen

55

to be fair up here in Amatina, don't you agree?'

'You're sounding more and more like your brother every day,' Dunstan accused.

'I'm not like anybody. I'm my own man.'

Matt's shoulders slumped in sudden weariness. 'That's right, you are. I can see it. I guess it's me that's changing. Right now I guess I feel tireder than I ever remember.'

It was an extraordinary admission coming from a man of this caliber. He stood staring across at Kurt who was speaking with a towner, and Gene almost felt a vague twinge of sympathy. Life could be no bed of roses for the sheriff of Amatina at the moment, he realized. Apart from all his regular concerns, Dunstan had the added burden of not knowing what Kurt might be hatching now he was free and full of bitterness. How could he know? Gene didn't know himself.

He heard himself say, 'Maybe you should get some rest, Sheriff.'

'That might be the best suggestion I've heard all day.'

Dunstan moved off slowly, the mob respectfully parting to let him through, a solitary man walking out his destiny. Gene raised his eyes to the southern hills, blue and smoky in the far distance. He was thinking of Diablo, missing the spread, the day to day routine, the seeming normalcy of it all compared with what was unfolding here.

He was fast beginning to suspect he was wasting his time in Amatina. He glanced across at Kurt, standing tall and defiant with arms folded as he watched Dunstan's receding figure with hard cold eyes. How did you help a man who didn't want it?

The meeting of the Amatina For County Seat committee found it hard to believe the change in the commander. Most had been present at the council chambers earlier to witness Brogan's extraordinary breakdown, had watched him led away like someone suffering a brain seizure which had left him bewildered, stumbling and incoherent.

Yet here he was at the meeting hall, calm, clear-eyed and as eloquent as ever as he reminded them of the reason he was visiting, of the common goal all were bent on achieving.

'We have every advantage over our chief rival for a town patent in Fremont City,' Brogan reminded crisply, clear-eyed and totally lucid, 'other than in the almost abstract area of perception. You realize what I'm saying, don't you, gentlemen?'

Heads nodded. Some understood, others did not.

'Well might you wonder at my neglecting ranch business and personal interests to engage the brigade in the pursuit of human offal like Wild Bob, originally from Diablo as I might remind you all,' he went on. 'It's really quite simple. I have it on good authority that it is the ongoing perception of Amatina as a town soft on outlaws and rustlers and all their heinous ilk that is causing confusion and delay with the town patent commission, and I am utterly committed to doing all in my power to destroy that perception by cleaning up these vermin any way I can at whatever cost is necessary.'

He paused to take a slug of water from a tall glass and stared intently from man to man in turn.

'And just in case any among you entertains the notion that I do not include the cess-pit of Diablo and that murdering Taggert whom the authorities saw fit to parole against all logic and decency, then let me disabuse you of that idea here and now. It's us or them, fellow citizens. Law and decency versus crime and corruption. I shall carry the fight to the enemy and you will support me all the way through to our ultimate goal, namely a law-abiding valley with Amatina elevated to its rightful status as county capital. Please tell me if I'm wrong, I really value your opinions.'

He interpreted their silence as agreement. Many did agree, but those who didn't lacked the nerve to speak up. Every man present wanted the huge commercial and political advantages that would accrue to Amatina should it achieve the status of county seat, but none saw the struggle in the 'people versus the outlaws' context that this man painted it. Privately most regarded the commander as an extremist, but if he was the extremist who could get them what they most desired then tacitly at least they were prepared to sit back and allow him to do it his way.

Some claimed he was crazy, living alone in a church. Maybe he was. But it never felt crazy here for Matt Dunstan, with multicolored shafts of soft light sifting down from the high stained-glass windows and heavy drapes and old timber pews seeming to absorb and mute the sounds of the street.

The street.

It was where he made his living. It was as wide as the West itself and any man who walked it with a star on his vest did so with death at his shoulder, even here on Diamond Street, Amatina, which he'd tamed over the years.

Or almost.

Despite recent outbreaks of outlawry and rustling in the more remote regions of the valley he'd been highly satisfied with the way his town had been operating for the best part of a year, ever since he'd kicked out the crooked gamblers and jailed several notorious troublemakers and hell-raisers. In truth, he'd considered Amatina an all but trouble-free town under his full control, until some anonymous official hand in a distant courthouse had signatured a parole authority enabling a dangerous man who'd once been a friend to walk free and head directly back to his old stamping ground.

The proven charge of murder brought against rebel rider Kurt Taggert had destroyed their friendship and given birth to ugly rumors of rivalry over a woman and whispered allegations that an anti-Diablo faction comprising Judge Pooley, Commander Brogan, and last and most alarmingly, Matt Dunstan – had withheld or juggled evidence and even indulged in jury-tampering in order to secure Taggert's conviction.

The very fact that the Taggert case had been recently reviewed resulting in his being paroled years ahead of his time, convinced many that there must have been something suspect in how that trial had been conducted, raising questions about Dunstan's integrity again.

These matters had weighed heavily on the lawman over recent days, as did the clash at the courthouse.

But all his concerns miraculously vanished the moment he stepped through his arched doorway into the stillness and the feel of big airy spaces. It was his refuge and never failed him.

He straightened and felt stronger as he closed the heavy maple door firmly and crossed the vestibule which he'd left unchanged when converting the former Church of God into his quarters.

He climbed the narrow arched stair to the former choir loft, shucking jacket and gun rig *en route*. The loft was now a parlor overlooking the shadowed nave, in back an alcove containing the bed he rarely shared with anyone anymore.

The way he figured, if a man couldn't take the lonesome life he had no business wearing a star.

No business wearing a star?

An unfortunate choice of phrase, Sheriff. Think of something else. Like the mellow smoothness of that first fine shot of The General's Own malt whiskey which he poured for himself here at the end of his every ten-to-twelve hour day behind the badge.

He actually smiled as he toted bottle and glass to

his favorite chair, swallowed half the drink in one hit, settled back. It always took a time to unwind and today had proved more testing than most with its mix of a shooting play, the always unsettling arrival of the Militiamen followed by the almost serious incident at the council chambers, plus the continuing unsettling presence of an ex-con ex-friend and five guns from Diablo.

Matt sighed and closed his eyes, blanking his mind, refusing to permit any of his private demons to trouble him tonight.

It would astonish the Amatina man in the street to learn that his sheriff was sometimes prey to secret troubles and guilts, some of which had disturbed his days and nights for a decade and more.

Matt Dunstan presented an image of the solidly reliable law enforcer who was on top of his job more than ever. He was reappointed year after year without a hitch and, despite some lingering old rumors and whispers, was widely regarded as the perfect man for a dangerous job.

Once he had actually been that man, and he missed the old Matt Dunstan the way he might a true friend. A friend, for example, such as Kurt Taggert had once been.

He scowled and took another swallow.

Blank the mind, Sheriff. Blank the mind and pour another. Thanks, Sheriff, good thinking. . . .

He must have dozed. He wasn't aware of a soft rain falling, causing the window light to dance and ripple on the walls. Drifting hazily he was dimly aware of water beginning to gurgle and chortle in the downpipes until the sounds formed into a regular rhythm and he opened his eyes, realizing someone was knocking on the door.

He cursed softly.

Everyone knew the church house was sacrosanct. By the time he quit work each day, whatever time that might be, he could find refuge here knowing he wouldn't be disturbed unless in the event of a real emergency.

He sat waiting for the sound to be repeated. His educated ears detected no sounds of riot, gunplay or some fool galloping his cayuse down the main stem to win a wager.

The knocking came again, light yet insistent. What was the betting it was something to do with Brogan's visit? he thought testily as he headed downstairs. Maybe tonight would be the time he would finally lose all patience with the man and put him in his place. Maybe.

Crossing the gloomy vestibule he could see the outline of somebody through the glass doors, a slender figure of average height. A woman, maybe. Tiredly, he half-smiled. A man could always hope.

He opened the doors to confront Tessa McNair, the former lover he hadn't seen in an age. She was standing there sheltering under a brolly looking every bit as lovely and composed as if they'd been together just yesterday, not back in the distant past.

'Hello, Matt.' Her voice reached out effortlessly and unchanged by time. 'Any refuge from the storm to be found here tonight?'

CHAPTER 5

GO OR STAY

Brogan was seething with wounded vanity as he led his brigade out of South Street the following morning, heading for the bridge and the still-fresh trail of notorious Wild Bob. Accustomed to being seen off by a goodly crowd on such occasions, the brigade had left almost unnoticed today due to overnight developments which had snatched focus away from the man-hunters from Buffalo Range almost totally.

Of course, it would have been out of character for Brogan to have left without ranting against the reappearance of the woman whose love affairs with former friends Kurt Taggert and Matt Dunstan was setting the gossips' tongues wagging afresh all over town.

'A whore co-habiting alternately with our best and our worst?' he'd speculated spitefully at a closed meeting with his inner circle of staunch supporters of the Citizens' Committee before leaving. 'I tell you Babylon never witnessed lust and depravity on such a scale as was seen here ten years ago, and now it seems we are expected to endure a reprise of it all. And just ask yourselves this. What will this grotesque state of affairs do to our standing with the patents office – though you might well ask what standing do we have left now anyhow? Are we going to allow outlaw Charlie Taggert's outlaw son and his Diablo henchmen to drag us into the mire yet again with so much hanging in the balance?'

Charlie Taggert was what it was all about. Years earlier when Brogan was sweeping the gangs out of the valley and gaining fame as far away as Washington for the swashbuckling way he went about it, he'd unwisely invaded the Diablo region only to be outsmarted, out-fought and eventually brought down to humiliating defeat by the Taggerts and their Diablo henchmen, whose aim in life was to live free by their own rules and resist any threat to that freedom no matter from where it might come.

Diablo had been the commander's greatest defeat. He'd enjoyed many other triumphs in the years since but humiliation still rankled.

Brogan had always insisted that, before he hung up his spurs, and either before or after Brandaman Valley's Amatina achieved its proper recognition, he would have to clean out that rat's nest for the good of the valley, and in so doing erase that old shame and stain on his record.

In the meantime he had to be content with running down bloody-handed Wild Bob and taking every opportunity to whip up public sentiment against the old enemy as represented by Charlie Taggert's formidable sons.

He believed he was making headway in that direction as he quit town, but believing didn't necessarily make it so.

The town had other things on its mind today and even as the brigade clattered across the bridge with its banner flapping bravely from its staff, wide-eyed matrons, cowhands, storekeepers and the regular battery of porch rockers and good old boys were being treated to the spectacle of Tessa McNair strolling past Goodfellow's store escorted by Matt Dunstan and Kurt Taggert. Both of them! To listen to the commander you'd reckon those two men were on the verge of setting up a duel to the death.

This was meat to fuel the gossips' appetites for days to come, but other onlookers were far less fascinated or approving.

'I reckoned I'd see everythin'.' muttered lean Bo Treece, perched on the porch railing of Jack's Keno Parlor in the shade. 'Can you tell me why them two ain't pacin' it off for a gundown, pard?'

Gene's clean-shaven face was blank. He'd been a kid when Tessa McNair apparently dumped the sheriff for his brother just prior to Kurt's being arrested, charged and eventually found guilty of a murder that he knew he'd never committed.

He'd been aware Tessa had maintained correspondence with Kurt throughout his prison term but had never expected to see her again, much less here and now in Amatina. He reckoned Kurt must have contacted her again upon his release and so she'd come to Amatina to join him.

He'd been on edge ever since Kurt's release. Now despite his outward calm, he was both edgy and angry.

The tension between Kurt and Dunstan had been high even before the woman's arrival. Mightn't she provide the perfect fuse to touch off the explosion? What could she be thinking?

Matt Dunstan had already received his answer to that very question, but Kurt Taggert was hearing it for the first time as the trio took seats on the law office porch while Deputy Lomax hustled about fixing coffee and pretending not to eavesdrop.

'I always felt badly about what happened to you as you know, Kurt,' Tessa stated gravely. 'You might as well know now I also always kept in touch with Matt as well as with you, I suppose out of some sense of guilt. But I never intended seeing either of you again until I heard you'd been paroled and had come back here instead of going home.'

She paused to smile at Deputy Lomax as he placed the cups on the bench. After taking a sip she touched the corners of her mouth with the tip of a lace handkerchief.

'I feared the worst immediately,' she continued. 'I still do, which is why I came back and contacted you both. We have to talk and work our way through this, painful though it must be for all of us. I felt responsible but never guilty for destroying your friendship and for what followed as a direct result. I know you both better than I know anyone, know what could happen here if someone ... perhaps me ... doesn't do something to pour oil on the waters ...'

She reached out and took both men by the hand, to the delight of passers-by who'd stopped to stare.

'Kurt, Matt, none of us is young anymore. It's all right for the young lovers to be hot-headed, jealous and even crazy if they will. But look where that led us. Surely neither of you can be planning to repeat past mistakes, and if you should do so I swear I shall never see either of you ever again. Never even think of you or care. That is why I'm here, why I came. Are you listening to me? Do you understand?'

It was difficult to tell if they did or not the way they traded stares, both tight-lipped, watchful, neither giving anything away.

Tessa had shared several months of a valley winter with Matt Dunstan prior to Taggert's arrival from the south with a played-out bunch and a bullet hole in his leg requiring medical attention.

Tessa, a nurse by profession, was doing several hours a day helping old Doc Blinx at the time.

Kurt Taggert would never forget that meeting. He limped into the surgery on Coyote Street with a three-day stubble, a leg strapped up in linen and rawhide and cursing from the pain when she demanded he stop swearing and coolly informed him that he smelt like a cesspool.

It was love at first sight.

Her hair was pure gold and her skin like milk, and she wore a plain starched uniform that had no hope of concealing the lines of the finest figure he'd ever seen.

These were the superficials. But it had been her intense femininity and the way she could look at a man and make him feel like king of the rangeland that was unique, something he'd never encountered before and knew he never would again unless he seized the moment.

They made love one week later and Taggert's best and worst period of his hard-lived life unfolded before him. He cared that they were cheating on Matt, but nothing could have stopped him. When Dunstan found out about the affair their friendship – always seen as odd by purists – ceased to exist. Taggert knew he could survive that if he must, but the romantic triangle remained the talk of the town until the night badman Kyle Clanton was killed on the back streets of Amatina and Kurt Taggert was arrested and charged with the murder by Sheriff Matt Dunstan.

Ten years ago. Ten years of enforcing the law on the streets of Amatina for Dunstan; the living hell of Yuma for Taggert; the comfortable uninvolved life as a banker's mistress in Nebraska for Tessa McNair, with just the letters she wrote to each man every month to connect her with the most remarkable period of her life.

Seated in silence now both men knew the

FIVE GUNS FROM DIABLO

woman was driven by the best motives. Why would
she come back unless she still cared for them
both?

But as for forgiving and forgetting, surely there
was a limit to how far a proud man could bend
backwards, even for somebody like her.

'Please at least consider it,' Tessa was pleading
until diverted by the arrival of the young man from
the eatery across the way, sporting a vivid red shirt
and a tied-down Colt .44.

' 'Scuse me, gents, ma'am,' said Johnny Ramble.
He winked at Kurt, rolled his eyes in appreciation
of the woman's beauty, then added: 'Kurt, Gene
sends a message. Says he wants to talk to you
tonight, six o'clock at the Palace. That OK by you?'

'Sure,' Kurt replied, around his cigar. 'Is he with
you over yonder?' Ramble nodded.

Kurt said, 'How come he didn't come over and
ask me himself?'

Ramble shot a sideways glance at Tessa before
answering.

'How can I put it, Kurt? Right now – and I
reckon I know Gene well as anyone – I'd say he
ain't feelin' all that sociable.'

'Let me guess,' Kurt said irritably. 'This is about
Tessa, keerect?'

'Hell, I'm just the messenger boy, Kurt. Will you
meet with is all I need to know.'

Kurt nodded and the man headed back across
the street, as slick and light-footed as a tango-
dancer.

'I hope I'm not causing trouble between you

and Gene, Kurt,' Tessa worried. 'That would be the last thing I'd want. I was always very fond of your brother.'

'Me too. But by Judas he can be ornery and prideful when he wants, damned if he can't.'

'It's called growing up,' Dunstan put in. 'And that young feller has done a damn fine job of it, considering all he's had to tote.'

'Don't start, lawman,' Taggert warned. 'My goin' to prison and leaving the kid to run things to home wasn't my doing if you'll recall.'

'I suppose you still reckon it was mine?'

'If the hat fits!'

'Please, don't start,' Tessa pleaded, her hopes fading fast as she glanced from one to the other. Matt wore an expression she'd seen on his face before, when moving in to break up a saloon brawl with his fists, a baton or his gun if needs be. Kurt's Taggert-blue eyes were the color of ice. He appeared to be measuring Dunstan for a coffin.

Gene Taggert sat in the porch shade of the Brandaman Valley Fast Freight office mid-morning the following day. He was dressed for the trail. A block distant at the Champion livery stable on Flub Lane they would be feeding and watering his horse in readiness for the journey south. Maybe he should be gone by now. But he wanted to take just a few quiet minutes to be certain he was making the right decision. It was OK for Kurt to act on impulse but someone had to be the steady one.

He couldn't help but grin at that.

He sounded like someone's maiden aunt. Sure, he and his brother had always been regarded as 'horses of a different stripe' and he supposed that was still the case.

Kurt had been sore last night when he learned of their plans to return to T-2 and Diablo. Too bad. He'd been working overtime to prevent a show-down between his brother and Dunstan, but knew when he was licked. If there'd been any chance of reconciliation it had gone out the window when Tessa McNair showed. It was like trying to get kids to quit playing with firecrackers and they switch to dynamite.

Amatina looked peaceful today, he mused, leaning back in the comfortable rattan chair. Wagons rolling by, matrons with baskets over their arms checking out the store windows. Indeed, on days like this it was easy enough to imagine the town as the county capital with all the increase in prestige, trade and development that that honor would bring.

If the commander could just stop chasing hellions long enough to give the town patent process his full attention it might easily achieve its goal before year's end.

He didn't hear the buggy approaching until it drew to a halt before the steps.

'Good morning, Gene.'

He stared up at the driver. He remembered Tessa McNair as a vividly beautiful woman attending his brother's trial every day at the courthouse years ago. She appeared virtually unchanged in a long-sleeved white blouse, divided skirt and tan boots, while that smile could still hit a man like a cattle prod.

He removed his hat as he came erect, sober and formal as he moved to the railing.

'Hello, Tessa.'

'My, I can't believe how you've changed, Gene.' She slid along the glove-leather seat and patted the space she'd made. 'I'm taking a run out to the Blue Hole for old time's sake. Care to join me?'

The invitation seemed spontaneous and impulsive although Gene doubted it was either. He sensed purpose behind her smile but resisted it. It had been a tough session with his brother last night. He wanted Kurt to go home with him but he'd refused. Instead his brother had pressed him to remain on here with him for just a few more days while he 'got a few things straightened out.' He'd not identified what those things might be although Gene reckoned it had to with Kurt's new role as a sleuth.

Each day the other was to be seen talking to people on the streets, in bars, at Midge Riddle's, the Drumhead, the First Chance or the Palace. He wandered around Poor Town quizzing bums and asking questions about a night far back in the past that most folks had all but forgotten.

'Lookin' for the killer... what else?' was his explanation when questioned. But nobody seemed to know if that was his genuine purpose or if he was simply putting on a big show to convince Amatina that they'd jailed an innocent man.

'Sooner or later something's gonna give, Gene,' he insisted. 'There are people here who were still around the night Clanton was killed, someone sure knows something. And when I find what I'm looking for I'm going to need men I can rely on to back me up when I go to Dunstan. It'd be fine to have you and the boys standing by.'

'No way,' had been Gene's response.

Now suddenly Tessa McNair was inviting him to go buggy-riding. Maybe she and Kurt had gotten together and figured he might respond to her appeal where he'd rejected his brother's.

No chance of that.

He'd made a decision and, like always, would stick to it.

Still, a little time in her company could scarcely be time wasted, he reflected. For she had been involved with both Kurt and Dunstan when his brother's world caved in and could maybe shed some light on those long-ago events leading up to that historic trial of The People *vs.* Kurt Taggert.

So he let her coax him a little more before shrugging and climbing up alongside. She wheeled the mare away expertly and he leaned back and tried to pretend this was an everyday kind of thing to be doing as their dust drifted back over the staring street.

They didn't talk much during the five-mile drive to the deep bend in the Little Shiloh known as the Blue Hole. He'd come out here once with Tessa and his brother just before the Clanton killing. He'd developed a crush on his brother's woman, but then just about every male in Amatina had always been at least a little in love with Tessa McNair.

He wondered if Kurt or Dunstan were still in love with her, or she with either or both of them. He was all for romance but didn't pretend to understand anything as complicated as this.

They sat side by side on a smooth rock watching fish make breath rings on the surface of the water while the horse cropped grass between the willows. Tessa asked a lot of questions and he did his best to answer them honestly. Did he believe Kurt had killed Clanton? He really didn't know. Did he suspect that somewhere around mid-trial Matt Dunstan might have submitted to pressure of one kind or another and ceased supporting his brother, thereby allowing the prosecution to secure its conviction? Could be.

She began another question but Gene held up his hand.

'My turn,' he said firmly. 'You know or knew Dunstan better than anybody, Tessa. He always struck me as straight as a die. But he was in love with you and Kurt grabbed you away from him. You tell me if you reckon he'd have been sore enough or mad enough to see a chance to take Kurt out of that picture, and took it.'

Tessa looked away. A heron had floated down onto a limb across the way, light as a zephyr. She seemed absorbed by the bird but in truth was considering his big question gravely.

She turned to him directly.

'I don't know, I really don't. I had suspicions at the time, but considering Matt's strength of character, and with no evidence to the contrary, I had to decide that he couldn't do such a thing ... probably.'

He nodded.

Helpful maybe but hardly conclusive.

He rose, ready to leave now. But she reached up and touched his hand.

'I wish you'd stay on in town, Gene. Kurt needs you.'

'No he doesn't. He never did. He or the old man. They were always different from me. Kurt still is. I'm heading back tomorrow and the boys can ride with me or stay if they want.'

'I hope you're not making a mistake.'

'Wouldn't be the first time.'

'Well, at least I'm glad we had this chat, Gene. Your brother told me you'd grown into a strong man, and I can certainly see that is so.'

'Kurt said that?'

'You seem surprised.'

'Not really.' He placed a hand under her elbow to assist her back up the bank. 'Sorry I can't stay, but I'm going to feel better if you're here to look out for him.'

'That's why I came back,' she replied, looking straight ahead. 'To look out for Kurt.'

'What about Dunstan?'

'Matt can look after himself. It's Kurt I love.'

That admission almost tempted him to stay on. But he knew he wouldn't. He rarely changed his mind once it was made up, if ever.

Dunstan drank alone. Her photograph was before him and the night seemed a hundred hours long.

It was over.

She'd told him so but he still wouldn't believe it. Could not. He'd lived in hope for ten years, so much so that it was part of him now. He thought about Kurt and Kyle Clanton and knew why he felt so old.

'I thought it'd be different, Tess, if we ever got to meet again,' he murmured in the semi-darkness he favored now. 'You and me . . . do I know how to just let you go. . . ?'

The council chamber's clock struck one. He knew he should get to bed, but knew he wouldn't.

CHAPTER 6

BLOOD IN BOBCAT ALLEY

The horseman burst from the moon shadows of the bluff to go careening across the stretch of open plain at a laboring gallop.

Wild Bob glanced back. No sign of them now. But he wouldn't relax until he reached the Little Shiloh some ten miles to the south-west. Beyond the river lay the Black Rock Hills and the old sanctuary of Diablo country.

The lathered bay leapt a deadfall and staggered before recovering balance. The rider cursed viciously as he shot another glance over his shoulder.

Far back along the track he'd taken out of the shadows, he glimpsed movement.

He hadn't shaken them at all.

They were still hammering after him.

Brogan!

He couldn't believe he'd been careless. Brogan's Brigade had been pressing him hard all the way down valley from Heron Lake for two days and nights before they'd veered off into Amatina to resupply. He should have known they hadn't quit the chase; knew he would have kept running hard, but for last night's chance meeting with the meat-hunter returning to camp – damn him!

The hunter had told him of the brawl at the council chambers and how Brogan had suffered some kind of attack. 'Like he'd been kicked in the head by a mule,' as he'd put it.

The outlaw had needed rest desperately, his horse even more. So he'd camped on a ridgetop only to lapse into an exhausted long sleep. He awakened many hours later to sight a large bunch of riders heading along his tracks for the ridge beneath a familiar fluttering banner, with a tall bearded figure riding lead.

How could a man be such a fool?

The badman shook his shaggy head and concentrated fiercely on the trail ahead. He squinted through straining eyes and calculated he was about a mile closer to the river. He looked back. They were still coming yet seemed in no great hurry now. And were his eyes deceiving him or were they fewer than before?

Imagination!

Just ride and think of the Black Rock Hills and the thousand places there to hide, as he and old Charlie Taggert had done in the wild days before they nailed Charlie, and Diablo had somehow turned almost respectable.

He raked horsehide with spur and the horse briefly picked up its gait.

Overhead the stars were a tangled net of fire, dimmed now and then by a fluttering cloud. He ducked beneath a low-reaching branch of a dead tree and winced as the pain in his shoulder grabbed him. He'd stopped a slug in the stage hold-up outside Silvertree and was still bleeding. He shook his head as the miles ahead shrunk from maybe eight to five or six. The horse was blowing hard but still holding its own with the pursuers, and the fugitive was imagining he could scent the river mere moments before he jerked upright in the saddle and hipped around wildly.

Something whispered past high overhead. A moment later he heard the distant whipcrack of a rifle.

His head jerked right where a broken-backed ridge reached out onto the plain. Had he caught a gunflash from the corner of his eye up there? Impossible. The bastards were still in back of him.

An orange spurt of bore flame flared hotly against the dark of the ridge and the horse grunted and staggered as the bullet slammed home.

Wild Bob couldn't believe it. He refused to believe that Brogan could have spotted his camp-site while he slept, had accurately predicted his run-out route for the river then sent men on ahead beyond the ridge to lie in wait in ambush when he came running across the plain like a Ute fleeing the Pony Soldiers. He refused to believe any of it until the horse staggered on the impact of a high-powered bullet. The animal stood on its nose and sent him flying over its head to hit and roll for a bruising fifteen feet before he could stop.

The sky was filled with red dust and he couldn't see what he was shooting at. Two slugs hummed close and he began to run, sobbing with pain and rage. The looming silhouettes of ghosts on horseback emerged abruptly through the red mist. He lurched to a halt, triggered twice and saw a hat go sailing through the air. He grinned like a dog wolf. Next thing he knew his face was in the sand and there was pain in his body and a roaring sound in his ears like a dam burst.

A voice seemed to come from a vast distance, hoarse, triumphant.

'It's him all right, Commander. They said he couldn't be caught but we got Wild Bob! Yeehahhh!'

Then, as rough hands rolled him onto his back: 'He's shot up plenty, Commander. What'll we do with the varmint?'

The answer seemed to come from on high like the voice of an Old Testament prophet. 'Not the courts this time. I'm taking no chance on this one doing a little time then returning to mock us like that other Diablo scum. Fetch me a rope!'

'I'd give up my front seat in hell to know if you're

81

bluffin', Diablo,' said the one-legged gambler.

'It'll cost you to find out,' replied Bo Treece, holding his cards close to his chest. 'Bet or fold.'

Standing in back of their partner to watch the game after losing the last of their folding money in the upstairs game above the First Chance, Ramble and Carlaw rolled their eyes at one another.

Treece was bluffing on one miserable pair of twos!

Across at the little bar, Dobbs sat munching nuts and drinking beer as he rolled his eyes romantically at a hard-faced chippy with tinsel and spangles in her hair. Dobbs had run short of both money and interest in the game long ago. Ramble and Carlaw felt the same. All had reached a stage where the attractions of Amatina were starting to pall and all were beginning to hope Gene was serious about heading homewards in the morning.

'Yours and up a dollar,' said the gambler.

'Your dollar and up five,' Treece replied, and Ramble and Carlaw looked at the ceiling.

The one-legged gambler puffed out his cheeks, drummed on the table, stared balefully at Treece.

Treece looked at his pair of twos then back to the gambler. Now Treece was purposely sporting the desperate look of a loser sitting on a pair of twos.

The gambler was not about to be fooled with that look. He knew a clever double-bluffer when he met one. He threw his two pairs of court cards down in a temper and quit the table.

Treece raked in his winnings and grinned up at his friends.

'That geezer doesn't know a triple bluff when he sees one. What say we go find Gene.'

Quitting the First Chance in high spirits as Treece good-naturedly split his winnings, the bunch made its way across the street for the Drumhead. A bulky figure in a poncho called a warning and they propped mid-street to allow a freighter's wagon to roll past, piled high with wet buffalo hides.

'Mmmm! That smell,' Dobbs said, inhaling deeply. 'Reminds me of a gal I used to know once.'

'Everything reminds you of a girl you used to know,' said Carlaw, grinning.

'Well, you sure as hell don't.' The blocky Dobbs laughed, punching him hard on the shoulder and causing him to stagger.

They were greeted at the saloon porch by an enormous black man sporting a foot-high black topper and stoking up a flaming tar barrel with a stick.

'Welcome to the Drumhead, brothers,' boomed the drummer. 'Best whiskey, best wheel and the very best chittlin's you'll find in all of Utah.'

'Never mind that bull dust, *compañero*,' Bo Treece grinned. 'Is our pard inside or ain't he?'

'Mister Taggert?' came the white-toothed reply. 'Sure 'nuff is. Say, howcome he ain't drunk and scatterbrained like you pecker-heads?'

'I reckon when the drummers start getting familiar a man knows he's been in a town too

83

long,' Carlaw opined as they jumped up the steps and swaggered inside.

'Amen to that,' said Johnny Ramble. 'Hey, there he is.'

They approached Gene who sat sharing a bowl of chittlings with a woman with a Southern accent who was trying to interest him in her while all he wanted to do was talk about a trial held way back in the past.

'You're wasting your time, honey,' she told Taggert as his pards hailed him boisterously. 'It's most always just pure waste of valuable time for a body to go poking around rehashing old stuff that everybody's forgotten about.' She reached out and tapped the back of Gene's hand. 'Your brother done it, Gene. The law said so, he did his time – or most of it, you got him back safe, so why don't you both just let it slide?'

'Were you at the trial?' Gene asked stubbornly.

That did it. The faded saloon flower shoved her bowl aside, got up and made for the bar. She considered Kurt Taggert's brother the finest specimen she'd met in years. But he was interested in only one thing, and it wasn't her.

'So?' Gene said, leaning back in his chair. 'Win or lose?'

'Lost,' lamented Dobbs. 'All but Bo, that is. How you holdin', Gene?'

'Getting low,' Taggert confessed. 'Guess I can hear Diablo calling.'

The ring of bronzed faces grinned eagerly. But Gene held up his hands palms-forward as he slid from his stool and tugged down his hat.

'But I got something to tend to first.'

They groaned.

'You said that yesterday and the day before that,' Johnny Ramble protested. 'What made you change your mind about headin' home of a sudden? And while we're at it, howcome you're gettin' so secretive in your old age anyway? Ain't we your pards, or what?'

Taggert just shook his head. He tossed a five-spot onto the counter. He walked out with a reassuring salute which didn't seem to reassure any of them.

He didn't blame them for showing skepticism. They'd all had a good run in Amatina. But now they were feeling the pull of home while he seemed to be wasting time.

But Gene was as anxious to get riding as were they. It was just that there was one last thing he must do first. See Kurt. They'd seen little of one another over recent days due largely to the fact that his brother was always busy wandering the streets buttonholing with anyone and everyone on just the single topic.

The murder and trial.

Gene figured he might act the same if it was him. But from an objective point of view he saw it all as mainly a waste of time now. If Kurt had been meant to turn up something he'd have done so by now. The trail of Clanton's killer was simply too old and cold.

He tracked him down at the back bar of the

Palace where he found him quizzing a black-bearded buffalo hunter who looked as if he couldn't remember last night, much less something that happened so long ago.

He got rid of the beard and bought two shots of the Green River whiskey for which the saloon was famous, didn't waste any time getting down to business.

'We're finally leaving, man. We all want you to come. How about it?'

Kurt's jaw set in that old stubborn way.

'This is my home until I get to find out who killed Clanton and how and why I got saddled with it, kid.'

'Don't call me kid.'

'Why not?'

'I don't call you pops.'

Kurt grinned and sipped his drink. They'd always had a tetchy kind of relationship due largely to the age gap. After their mother passed on and their father was shot down trying to rob an express office in Arizona, Kurt, then at the age that Gene was now, had taken on the responsibility of running the spread and rearing him to manhood. Kurt had never let him down, not once. But they were a man and a boy, with markedly different personalities, Kurt half wild as old Charlie Taggert had been, Gene strong, quieter and by most standards, straight.

'I got a feeling I'm getting close to smelling out something here,' Kurt said intently, tilting his glass and watching the light refract from it. 'Somewhere there's a jasper who put that knife into Clanton that night, and thinks he got away with it. A man can hide but he can't disappear. That night . . .' His voice faded and he shook his head.

Gene studied his brother.

'Y'know, Kurt, even after all this time you've never told me exactly what happened that time with you and Clanton . . .'

'You really want to know? I mean, would you believe me?'

'Try me.'

Kurt leaned back and began to talk more soberly and eloquently than Gene had ever heard him, so much so that as he got into his story it was as though he was really there with his brother ten years ago here in Amatina on a rainy night . . . down in Bobcat Alley hard by Poor Town, could smell the rain, the whiskey and the poverty. . . .

Kurt Taggert stood in the misting rain fingering a swollen jaw and sporting a black eye, a real shiner. His brawl earlier that day with Kyle Clanton had proved a genuine rafter-rattler up in the main gaming-room of the Palace until Matt Dunstan broke them up.

The Clantons and the Taggerts had always fought, always made up. Both clans lived on the shady side of the street in those days and even then vigilante leaders such as Commander Brogan had railed against their excesses and conducted largely futile campaigns to limit their mischief.

That night, after having been patched up by his

live-in lover, Tessa McNair, and learning he'd broken Clanton's arm in the fight, Taggert was overcome by boozy regret and was searching for the man to patch things up with him when he learned Kyle had just been seen cutting into Bobcat Alley, taking the short cut through the back streets to Poor Town.

Taggert hurried into the alley, which had a bad reputation for assaults and muggings, where reeling boozehounds and opium addicts from the slums often lurked with intent by night and by day.

The tall man rounded two dark corners and saw the figure sprawled across a broken crate, his chest a crimson mess. One look was all it took to tell him Kyle Clanton had been hacked to death with a knife.

A furtive rustling sounded beyond the pile of crates!

Taggert palmed his cutter and shouted: 'Freeze, you butchering bastard!'

He saw a dim silhouette moving away. He triggered once, twice, the grimed alley lighting up to the shimmering gunflashes.

Receding footsteps: step–drag, step–drag. Maybe he'd scored a hit, or could be it was just a limper.

He began reefing crates out of the way, then swung about as the back door of a hovel swung open, bathing the scene in light.

'B'Gawd!' a man croaked. 'Looks like someone's been done in and . . . hey, ain't that you, Kurt?'

One of the first to reach the scene was the sheriff.

'That's the story,' Kurt stated flatly, his vivid word-picture slowly dissolving from Gene's imagination as he stood and took out his tobacco. 'Motive, no witnesses, the whole Clanton clan bellowing for my blood. And, of course, Matt. He sure had no call to go easy on me, although he seemed to be backing me until around half-way through the trial, then buckled under. Of course Judge Pooley always hated my guts, and when Brogan showed up with his damned militia and a bunch of high-priced attorneys from Canyonville to make sure 'justice was done', why, I guess I was a goner long before they brought down their crummy verdict.'

He paused to light his smoke and shook out the match. He cocked one eyebrow.

'So?'

'The guy with the limp. Did you. . . ?'

'If I had a buck for every joker with a limp I've quizzed . . .'

Kurt broke off and shrugged. In that moment he appeared old and tired. But tough. His brother was one of the genuinely tough ones, Gene knew. Tough, mule-stubborn, and right now he looked as if he felt he'd talked too much. But Gene had one more question he wanted answered.

'Where did Tessa McNair stand at that time? I was too young to figure. Was she with you or the sheriff . . . or both of you?'

89

'She was with me. Had been for weeks. Just like she is now.'

'Do you reckon that. . . ?'

'Reckon not,' Kurt said, anticipating him. 'That bust-up made enemies out of me and Matt but he's still the straightest shooter I ever met. He'd never tamper with the law to get at a man . . . although there were times when I reckoned he had. Pooley would. And Brogan certainly threw everything he had into getting a conviction on account of he hates Taggerts and Diablo worse than a rat hates red pepper. But those pilgrims are too big to bring down or even say too much about. No. If I've still got a chance it's finding that geezer who jumped Kyle when he was drunk then stabbed him with his own big knife when he put up a fight. That's why I'm staying on in Amatina.'

Gene knew when he was licked.

He was tempted to stay on and maybe try and help out some more. But he knew he wouldn't. He just shook hands and made his goodbyes.

There was a spread to run down south, he reminded himself as he collected his friends and hit the street. As well, he'd also contracted to rent graze and water to a big trail herd making its way north out of Arizona heading for the meat packers beyond the valley. Men from Diablo might still be dubbed rustlers, gunmen and troublemakers as a legacy of their past. Yet over the years, with Kurt Taggert languishing in prison and his brother growing to manhood, T-2 Ranch had expanded and grown strong while the old hellraiser image

90

faded in the eyes of most, with a few major exceptions.

He wanted to get back to that life he'd shaped for himself. Couldn't wait for first light to come, when they'd kick the dust of troubled Amatina off their heels and take the trail home.

He was eager to get back quickly, yet still knew he would take the long way home through the Sheepherder Hills. He did it every single trip these days, yet still wasn't real sure why.

CHAPTER 7

CANYONVILLE

The marshal's office stood two blocks south of Canyonville's stage depot where the Amatina delegation alighted stiffly from their stage at the end of the rough journey across the Sabinosa Hills from Brandaman Valley.

The bustling farming and timber town lay ten miles east of the Sabinosas, laid out leisurely along both banks of one of the finest fishing streams in the territory.

A mile down the road stood undermanned Fort Ethan Smith which housed the small army garrison responsible for a vast area reaching north-east almost to Sevier Lake. Close by to the stockade was the fieldstone courthouse housing the 21st District Court.

The delegation of the Amatina Citizen's Committee weren't interested in courthouses, timber mills, exchange houses or any other big-town paraphernalia this visit. They had been assured an audience with the regional marshal and made their way directly to that big airy building without delay to find Thompson himself standing on the long gallery waiting for them.

The federal lawman was a tall, spare man who relaxed in his chair behind an uncluttered desk with hands locked behind his head while the mayor spelled out the reason for their visit.

Amatina was going to hell in a handbasket and they wanted the marshal to come and help solve their problems. That was the gist of their appeal and they really wanted to know what he was going to do about it.

He'd expected something along these lines, so Thompson was ready.

'Gentlemen,' he said, amiably yet firmly, 'we're aware of your difficulties, don't imagine we are not. The unexpected parole and return of a murderer . . . hardcases wandering your town . . . upset and uncertainty on every hand. Then of course there was that eventful visit by our old friend the commander, which raised one hell of a dust, or so I am led to believe.'

He paused to smile reassuringly.

'You see, we do understand. But!' He was emphatic as he raised a hand when several made to interject. 'But you really must understand our position. We here in Canyonville are responsible for enormous areas of territory and as always we don't have the resources necessary . . .'

He kept talking but lost most of them at that

point. The visitors from the valley had heard it all before. They understood that most likely resources were stretched, but couldn't they make this man understand just how difficult circumstances had become at Amatina? Didn't he realize they feared crisis coming if matters didn't improve?

The marshal was almost as efficient at dealing with supplicants as in enforcing the territorial laws, which was very good indeed. Eloquently and forcefully he supplied all the detailed reasons why he could not intervene in valley affairs at this time. He thought he'd made himself very plain but found out differently when he paused for a cup of coffee.

The mayor was red-faced and determined as he got to his feet to reiterate old arguments which he embellished with some of the new.

Their main concern, he explained forcefully, was that Kurt Taggert's return and the ominous presence of his Diablo riders in town might trigger off violence, considering Taggert's fierce resentment against his conviction and imprisonment.

And this wasn't all, the mayor insisted, without pausing for breath.

Taggert's release seemed to have fired up all the commander's old obsessions against lawlessness in general and Diablo in particular, dating back to not one but several failures by the brigade to impose its authority in that hold-out corner of the valley. He touched on Brogan's seizure, voicing the opinion that he considered the man to be teetering on the edge, raising grave concerns about both his state of mind and just what an obsessed man with his powers might do next.

'Then there is the sheriff . . .' he continued, but Thompson had heard enough griping for one day.

'Now don't start in complaining about the finest peace officer in five hundred miles, Mr Mayor. I won't hear of that.'

'Was and is the best, Marshal,' agreed the mayor. 'But we still have cause for concern. You must understand: a certain woman who was very much involved with the sheriff and Taggert and that whole ugly affair of ten years ago has returned to Amatina since Taggert's release. Now it appears that all the old volatility and uncertainty that surrounded those three people before might be bubbling to the surface again. This has led to a strengthening feeling in Amatina and amongst this delegation that Sheriff Durstan isn't the man he was, and that the man simply isn't coping with an admittedly thorny situation as he should.'

That was as far as they were allowed go. Thompson was a patient man but because his position was every bit as difficult as he maintained, he refused to debate problems he was unable to deal with at the moment.

The delegation left in a huff, they'd done previously. The marshal told his deputies he was glad to see the back of them – 'self-seekers and self-important nobodies to' a man', as he described them testily.

Yet later, as he considered a report on Amatina supplied by a representative of the district court in relationship to another unconnected matter, he found himself having sobering second thoughts.

It was impossible to analyse a situation clearly from this distance, but it did seem that the valley town just might prove to be a tinderbox if everything in the report and more of what the delegation had alleged was correct.

For the truth of the matter was that, for some time now, the marshal had felt himself reluctantly approaching the point of agreeing that something would eventually have to be done to curb Brogan's increasing excesses.

And what about Kurt Taggert?

That parole decision had come as a jolt. Experience told him the parole board rarely authorized a major cut of a prisoner's sentence unless new and compelling evidence was brought to light.

He stroked his chin. Taggerts, Diablo, militia, the sheriff, the McNair woman ... He shook his head, which was beginning to ache some by this. He was grateful when a deputy came in to tell him that somebody was missing some prime cows from the shipping yards. He needed a diversion; any diversion would do.

But the federal lawman knew Amatina would stick in his mind. He could only hope the town could keep its head above water until it received the county seat nod. He was sure this would happen eventually. He reckoned Amatina a certain choice providing no major trouble erupted there between now and then.

The sheriff appeared in the doorway of the livery stables.

'Catch my cayuse and saddle him up,' he told Chicken Pickles. In the adjoining lean-to he traded his coat for a slicker in case of rain, then buckled on a pair of spurs and paused to light up before returning to the barn where the liveryman was throwing a saddle over the back of his sturdy quarter horse.

'Not the best day to be ridin', Sheriff.'

'Make sure there are no wrinkles under that blanket.'

Pickles looked up sharply but didn't respond. It wasn't like Matt Dunstan to treat a man like a lackey. Still, everybody agreed the sheriff had been under plenty pressure recently. From gossip he'd heard, Pickles reckoned he had a fair notion of what might be the cause of this, but had no intention of trying to find out.

Main Street paused momentarily to watch soberly as the sheriff rode out, then went about its business. Thunder rumbled in the distance. Spring weather was always this way in the valley. Unpredictable. Just like the sheriff knew he was getting to be lately.

There were no pressing matters requiring his attention outside town today, and he wasn't a man who normally went riding without a purpose. He knew he was getting out in order to grab a fresh perspective on both the town and himself. Felt like he needed both badly.

Dunstan put the horse across the shallow crossing in the creek by the lightning-split beech. He headed up into the hills and was cheered by how good it felt just to be rocking along going noplace in particular with nobody watching his every damn move.

He knew folks were noticing the changes in him. He wasn't sure if he gave a damn. But wasn't not caring, in itself, a bad sign? Could be.

The going was slow but there was no cause to hurry. The higher he climbed the more strongly he felt he might be getting to clear some of the gray stuff out of his mind. As he gazed down through a scatter of live-oak he saw the widow's house and felt a twinge of guilt. Might stop by on the way back. Might. . . .

He reined in and dismounted on a grassy knoll. From here Amatina appeared serene and untroubled. Maybe it still was that way to most. He'd seen the town in that light himself until recent times.

A frown cut his eyes as he felt unwanted thoughts and names attempting to intrude. Brogan, Tessa, Kurt. . . .

At least Gene Taggert and his pards had left. Not that they ever caused much trouble, he had to concede. He liked young Gene, just as he'd once liked his brother. He sensed the younger Taggert was stronger even than Kurt, maybe stronger than just about anyone he knew.

He shook his head to clear it of all thoughts and the half-hour that followed left him feeling more relaxed than he'd been in days. While still in that fine mood he swung a leg over the quarter horse and took it down along the bridle trail. The wind-ing track came out by Gentry Street which he followed until reining in at the handsome white house with the flowering gardens.

Clara was in the garden as he knew she always was around this time. She greeted him gravely as he tied the horse up at the gate and joined her.

'Matthew. I haven't seen you in some time.'

He nodded and made small talk. After a time they went inside where the widow fixed coffee and brought out some ginger biscuits.

'Your favorites, Matt. I made them for you.'

He felt the tension beginning to build. She was a damned fine lady and he could do a lot worse. Maybe they might have gotten someplace had events not overtaken them. He wanted to believe he could still dominate people and shape events as he wanted. But doubts niggled. Tessa was in town. Kurt Taggert was all over the place asking ques-tions, poking into things, poring over transcripts of his trial at the courthouse.

He didn't know where the hell Brogan was or what he was doing these days.

And what was Matt Dunstan doing in the midst of all this? Playing the regret game, of course.

'You're not looking well, Matthew.'

He came out of his reverie and studied her. Clara Briet was a fine looking woman, calm, steady, rich. She cared for him and he'd always known it. There was a good life here for the taking. All he had to do was reach for it. But he'd never reached and knew he never would. Likely she knew it too.

'I'm fine, Clara,' he said, rising.

'It's her, isn't it?'

'Who?'

'Tessa McNair.' She'd never spoken that name in his hearing before. She looked into his face. 'When she returned recently, Matthew, she turned to Kurt Taggert, didn't she?'

'Damnit, Clara I don't—'

'I knew it immediately at the time. I saw it in your face.' She touched his arm. 'Matthew, that's not the end of the world. She loved you once but love doesn't always last . . .'

He had only a vague recollection of quitting the house some time later and returning the horse to Pickles' livery.

Although he didn't feel like it he stopped by at the jailhouse on his way home. It was a mistake. The deputies told him Brogan was back and the brigade was camped out at Medusa mine amidst mounting rumors that they'd hanged an outlaw someplace, then raised hell down south in the Diablo region.

That wasn't all.

The Citizens' Committee delegation had returned from Canyonville where they'd gone looking for help over his head without his knowledge, and hadn't got it.

But the clincher was that Kurt Taggert had told somebody that he felt he was getting close to uncovering just who did kill Kyle Clanton all those years ago, had even boasted about it to Deputy Lomax.

And he'd been with the McNair woman at the time.

Too bad the Black Hawk War of 1865–68 had already been fought and decided, Matt Dunstan thought cynically as he headed for his street. Today would have been a perfect day for that news to slug him as well.

It was coming on dark when he entered St Matthew's and closed the tall, stained-glass doors behind him. He waited for that familiar feeling of peace and security the place always gave him. It didn't come, hadn't done so for some days now.

Upstairs he splashed three fingers of bourbon into a glass before opening a drawer to take out a gilt-framed daguerreotype. By the dying light he studied the decade-old print showing a confident Matt Dunstan and a radiant Tessa McNair frozen in sepia-tinted time.

He leaned back and the big silences seemed to bear down on him. The nave was breathless, thick with flickering shadows. His voice was barely audible.

'Go home, Kurt. Take her – I can live with that. It's you she loves, not me and at last I've come to terms with that . . . I think. But let the trial and the verdict and all the rest of it lie, man . . . just plain let it lie. Maybe I can lose Tessa, but not everything. There's no way I'll let you take everything away from me. . . .'

He tipped his glass to his lips.

It was bitter whiskey he was drinking.

'See yonder, Colonel,' Trask said, pointing ahead. 'That's Crazy Woman Pass. No more than an hour's riding to the mine. I told you we'd make it by dark-down, didn't I.'

Slumped in his saddle a half-length ahead, the commander barely heard his gunman above the monotonous drum of hoofbeats. The sun was setting, burning away like an old fire in back of the loping cavalcade. Even had he heard his man it was doubtful he'd have taken one blind bit of notice. The brigade had ridden long and hard that day and Brogan had been in one of his darkest moods ever since quitting the Black Rock and Sheepherder hills to take them back up valley.

Brogan and his hardcase crew masquerading as vigilantes were returning from a failed mission to the Black Rock hills – Diablo territory.

The expedition into alien country had been the commander's impulsive notion, coming hard on the heels of the capture and murder of the outlaw Killane.

Flushed with the triumph of counting coup on a man with loose Diablo connections, and in the belief that Gene Taggert and his riders were still at Amatina, Brogan thought he saw an opportunity to do what he'd been unable to do before, namely to infiltrate the Black Rocks and attack the network of kin and friends of the Taggerts as first step in a campaign to bring the whole pocket of independence to ruin.

It hadn't played out that way. The T-2 ranch was a natural fortress set in the heart of a rugged region where Brogan's Brigade was the common enemy. Immediately Brogan's mission to beard the enemy in his den switched to a surveillance operation.

In typical Brogan style, he'd vented his fear and frustration on nobodies and bums. Nobody could figure what that might achieve, even if his men always enjoyed cutting up rough. But then, not even Trask seemed to understand very much of whatever the commander said and did these days while the rank-and-file were openly beginning to long for the old days when his mind was razor-sharp and he knew exactly whom to go after and how to bring them down.

But one thing even the greenest recruit understood was how the current campaign had ignited their leader, and who was responsible.

Kurt Taggert's parole had been the trigger.

It was Taggert's unexpected release and his pursuit of fresh evidence to support his call for a retrial that had seen Brogan immediately quit his giant ranch in mid-roundup and muster every available militiaman to deal with what he regarded as a Diablo revival.

His humiliating clash with the Taggerts in Amatina had only served to inflame all his malevolent hatred, which he'd appeased a little by bagging Wild Bob and sending him southward. To failure.

Now, riding slump-shouldered and silent, the leader seemed outwardly calm, yet Trask continued to study him closely. More and more the one-armed gunman found himself in the role of guardian, protecting his leader from bad judgment and excess.

But the day was now cool, they had the wind in their faces and it was only a few more miles to their proposed bedground at the old Medusa mine campsite up along the stage trail, which lay in easy reach of Amatina.

Suddenly Brogan seemed to realize exactly where they were. Without warning he hauled his big horse hard left and the company had no option but to follow.

'Where are we goin' now, Commander?' Trask wanted to know.

'The plain, of course.' Brogan sounded sharp and precise. 'To savor our great triumph.'

The line of riders traded glances. Nobody wanted extra miles. But nobody dared argue, not even Trask.

They sighted the first buzzards as they put the mesquite slopes behind them to reach the plain.

As they approached the shallow gullywash where spindly paloverdes drooped above gnarled thornbrush and coarse yellow grass, the birds rose in croaking angry clouds of flapping wings, with beaks and breasts stained with crimson.

A youthful brigadier hauled his sidearm and loosed a gunful of bullets overhead. One slug found a target. The yellow-necked turkey buzzard seemed to explode from within, scattering feathers over a wide area as it glided gracefully towards the rocks before slamming into them, head first and dead.

Scarcely anyone saw the bird fall. Every eye was drawn to what hung from the tree limb, something with a vaguely humanoid shape but so torn and bloated that it could have been an animal, gutted, disfigured and hung out to rot in the sun.

'Oh, yess!'

The exultation seemed to rise all the way up from Brogan's big military boots. He stood in his stirrup irons and pumped the darkening air with a gloved fist, his face animated again.

'Behold our triumph, militiamen!' he shouted. 'Our reason for being! And may God damn and blast every Diablo in this valley and condemn them to this dog's fate in this life and burning damnation in the next. Three cheers for the valley and its new county seat!'

Usually his outbursts drew unstinting approval from his followers. Not this time. No militiaman had had any brief for one-time Diablo rider Bob Killane and there'd been no regret in watching the desperado kicking and choking his life away on the end of a length of greasy rope slung over a paloverde limb. But it had seemed a minor victory at best. Surely this was a campaign to deal with the revived Diablo threat, not a dog hunt.

'Inspirational!' Brogan insisted. 'The crusade continues, my warriors. Today one miserable horse-thief, tomorrow . . . who knows? So be fierce and follow me once again on the path to glory! Charge!'

A dark and mottled mass, the cavalcade rushed away into the fast-falling night, their passage stirring the air and causing the corpse at the end of the rope to sway to and fro to the tick-tocking rhythm of the gibbet.

There was a full moon that night, marking the end of their third day back on the spread. It came up white over Coxcomb Hill then turned to gold, sheening the rooftops of house, barn, stables, outbuildings and shimmering the waters of the big old half-tank where a crew of naked drovers were sluicing away three weeks of sweat, trail dust, mud and rain.

The wind had risen just on dusk. It fingered the hillside trees and lifted a thin veil of dust off the back pasture beyond the bedded trail herd.

The mob from Arizona had arrived mid-afternoon. This had given the five three full days to pitch in and bring everything up to ship-shape on the T-2 in preparation for their arrival.

Gene had found the spread just as he'd left it. They had neighbors who kept an eye on things whenever they were absent. In any event, the T-2 could almost run itself most times. Their cattle were nearly all half-wild and accustomed to foraging, while hardly anyone bothered seriously about robbing people while they were away down in these parts any longer, not like they'd done in the good old days.

Outsiders mightn't believe it but the region with the notorious name had gotten to be one of the most law abiding places in Brandaman Valley, apart from the occasional all-in brawl, domestic upset or sixgun disagreement over a questionable brand.

Charlie Taggert had founded the then T-3 and financed its upkeep by rustling, bailing up stage-coaches and straight-out robbery under arms. His sons had taken part in some of these activities up until the day the law caught up with Charlie, leaving them to fend for themselves.

In those early years Diablo's bad rep was genuine and Gene and Kurt had stocked and restocked T-2 several times over with cattle whose brands would never stand too close a scrutiny.

After Kurt went to Yuma Gene fired the old light-fingered crew who couldn't learn new ways. He then signed up several boyhood buddies and set out to see if a man couldn't raise cattle and make a living without shooting people and getting shot at.

He reckoned he'd succeeded.

True, they were still regarded as gunmen and worse up north, but were astute enough to realize that Diablo would likely never acquire a completely clean slate even if they shaved their heads and donned the monks' habit.

Along with regular ranching they hunted and gentled wild cattle and horses, traded in most farm stock with the exception of sheep, and even got to visit Diablo most weekends with enough hard money in their Levis to have a real fine time.

There was no formal law in Diablo, which was how everyone liked it down here near the border. But self-administered home town justice could be

swift and sometimes brutally final if a man seriously transgressed. The strength of Diablo was its
cohesive tribalism which manifested itself fiercely
in times of emergency no matter who or what the
threat.

It was during one such conflict with a younger
but still dominant Brogan that Diablo and the
brigade had initially become mortal enemies.

Brogan came to the Black Rocks to apprehend a
Diablo horse-thief on behalf of Fremont's
marshal's office. Charlie Taggert had led the fight-
back which saw Brogan badly wounded, his
company defeated and his reputation as the
valley's favorite son set back on its heels. The feud
had simmered and flared into flame ever since.

Gene was feeling relaxed and easy tonight yet
was keenly aware of a tingling in his toes and a
certain kind of eagerness that suggested it was time
to get to town. Not for supplies, as they'd done
upon their return from Amatina, but rather
simply to have a good time – Diablo-style.

They left the Arizonans in charge an hour later
and Gene on his white led Treece, Carlaw, Dobbs
and Ramble down off the plateau, through the
timber, then out on to the lightly wooded uplands
which rolled away in gentle folds and timbered
curves all the way down to the town.

He felt good for the first time in weeks. Kurt and
Amatina seemed another world away tonight. He
was young, he reckoned some girls in town would
be glad to see him, and it wasn't until he declined
the offer to race the final five miles to town for a

dollar-a-man stake that he realized Amatina must have made him more sober and serious without his being aware of it before.

But looking back he reflected that it would be odd if he hadn't changed some. Kurt's release and return to Amatina had been dramatically unexpected, creating a highly charged atmosphere in Amatina compounded for all when it was realized Kurt planned on playing detective in the hope of clearing his name.

Gene had been there and seen his brother's single-mindedness strike sparks every day. His reaction had been a confusing sense of both pride and guilt. Pride because of the risks the other was taking, guilt because he'd never been dead certain in his own mind whether Kurt had been guilty or innocent of murder.

But the friction between the brothers had other sources and flashpoints. Before he was shipped out of Amatina in a lumbering gray wagon with YUMA daubed on its flanks in ominous black copperplate, Kurt had always treated him real fine, yet like a kid. Since his comeback he sensed his brother almost resented the fact that Gene had grown a mile, made his own friends and enemies and had improved the T-2 out of sight during his absence.

It was those kinds of thoughts that occupied him as they covered the last miles, which was the reason he didn't focus on something that had been annoying Dobbs, Carlaw and Treece over the last quarter-hour of their journey.

Johnny Ramble was fooling with his sixgun, a habit he tended to slip into at times.

'Hey!' Gene said sharply. 'What's all the clicking and slapping about, man? You turning into Billy the Kid or somebody?'

He grinned as he spoke but Ramble was sober as he replied:

'Just keepin' limber, is all.' He spun the .45 on his forefinger in a glittering arc, levelled the piece off, dry-snapped the trigger on an empty chamber. 'No sense in a man gettin' rusty these days.'

Gene frowned. 'These days? We're back home amongst the cows, or maybe you hadn't noticed.'

'Sure,' Ramble replied, staring ahead at the lights now glowing through the trees. 'But we'll be goin' back to Amatina sooner or later. And when we do, we'd better be limber.'

The others had caught up and were listening. Eli Carlaw frowned.

'Seems we still don't know what you're talking about, Johnny. Eh, Gene?'

'Keerect.'

'I'm talkin' about Kurt and the sheriff's woman and him playin' detective and that crazy old sunova Brogan fixin' to nail Kurt and all of us too while everyone else is walkin' on eggshells waitin' for the lid to blow. That's what I'm talkin' about. And that's howcome I'm makin' sure that I'll still know what end of a gun the bullet comes out of when we get up there and – hey! Ain't that little Jenny Tully off Whipple Creek?'

They were suddenly in the town and Ramble was

110

laughing like a kid as he heeled his way ahead, leaving Gene massaging the back of his neck and frowning. Then with a what-the-hell grin of his own he raked horsehide with bootheels and followed them for the main street.

They clattered noisily into the heart of a town where nothing ever seemed to change. Cowboys still raced their ponies down the main stem at full gallop, it still got overcrowded of a Saturday night, and the Diablo saloon was still the best place to get a cold beer.

The hours simply vanished as they swaggered from saloon to dance hall to eatery and back to the dance hall again: young men full of energy and high spirits who'd not seen any young-man brand of fun since Gene received his official letter of notification from the department of paroles up in Salt Lake City.

Gene Taggert didn't rate himself much of a dancer but he sure knew how to have a good time. Still. This seemed to surprise him. He guessed he'd been afraid recent events might have turned him into a killjoy and a sobersides, old before his time.

It was around eleven when five lithe men sporting broad-brimmed hats and any amount of artillery at last quit Daisy May's Fine Eats to make their reluctant way along the main street with the horse corral their ultimate destination.

The street was still roaring and there seemed to be more visitors than usual in town this Saturday night; drifters, red-faced farmers, strolling back-lot

111

families enjoying the sights while ancient sour-
doughs sat slumped on their porches chewing,
spitting and snapping their suspenders.

The bunch was passing Doc Keene's combined
barbershop and medical clinic when Gene
propped in mid-stride then took two steps back,
bumping into Dobbs, who cursed and puffed up
his chest.

'What's the big idea, cowboy? Why don't you
holler before you back up? You been drinkin'
mebbe? Ah swear ah'd jug you iffen we had a jug.'

Gene didn't reply. He was staring at the figure of
a girl standing in half-light and half-shadow under
the barbershop awning. Although he couldn't see
her clearly he was certain he knew her. Bo Treece
was the hawk-eye of the bunch, and he identified
her at a glance.

'I be damned, Gene. What's your sheepherder
gal doin' in this wicked old town at night all by
herself?'

Gene strode back and leapt up onto the porch.
The girl, wearing a head shawl and hugging
herself as though cold, lifted her head and he saw
that it really was the sheepman's daughter. And she
was crying.

CHAPTER 8

NORTH FROM DIABLO

'Come in, honey,' Tessa said. She was tall and slender in a snug-fitting shirtwaist with its blue collar turned up and a smoothly pleated beige skirt. Her hair hung loose to her shoulders and Kurt felt it brush lightly against his face as he bent to kiss her. She looked him up and down and seemed to find everything she saw to her liking. 'I really didn't think you'd come.' She smiled. 'I thought you might have bumped into somebody new with a limp, which meant I mightn't have seen you all day.'

He gave her a crooked grin.

'Are you hinting I'd rather spend time harassing some ugly polecat with a wooden leg than take you to lunch?'

'Oh, is that where we're going, Mr Taggert?'

It certainly was. Midge's special today was ribs, and like everything that mite-sized little lady put together, they were first class.

'Well,' Tessa said soberly when they'd reached the coffee and cigarette stage while doing their best to ignore all the curious stares, 'I almost hate to ask, but any luck?'

Kurt shook his head. No. He was on the streets even longer and later this week, asking questions, talking with friends and strangers. He'd been seen all over the town, even down in Poor Town, where daily life seemed roughly about as comfortable as Yuma.

He'd interrogated men with gout, arthritis, missing legs, paralysis and sufferers from all the different skeletal injuries man could sustain getting thrown off horses. The sum total of all that talk and worn shoe-leather – nothing.

Tessa patted his hand. 'In that case, it might be time, Kurt.'

He regarded her suspiciously. He'd grown tetchy and at times prickly as the days went by, but rarely with her. With Gene and the boys back in Diablo she was about the only person in this man's town he felt he could trust.

'Time for what?' he demanded even though pretty certain he knew what she was thinking.

He was right.

'Time to quit, of course.' She squeezed his hand as he made to argue. 'Honey, I've bad feelings about the way things are going. The whole town is walking on eggshells these days and now there's

114

talk in the paper today that Amatina might not become the seat after all.' She spread her hands. 'Matt has changed so he hardly seems to want to talk anymore, and there are all kinds of disturbing rumors about the militia making trouble down valley, even stories that they hanged somebody. You're all alone here now and I think you'll have to give up the hope of clearing yourself and just, well, leave.'

He considered his answer. Everything she'd said was true. Everything, that was, other than it was time for him to quit.

He wasn't quitting. He was about to say so when he saw Tessa glance up sharply as someone shoved through Midge Riddle's creaky old door. He turned his head to see Matt Dunstan making their way, removing his hat.

Kurt's eyes widened. He'd only seen the sheriff at a distance over the past couple of days. Up close he appeared drawn and gray, as though he'd been drinking too much or maybe not getting enough sleep.

'Tessa, Kurt.' Dunstan was formally polite. He indicated an empty chair and both nodded. He sat, placing his black hat on the damask cloth. 'I'm glad you're both here as there's something I need you both to hear.'

'Sounds important, Matthew,' Tessa said.

'Sure it's important,' Kurt declared lightly. 'You want me to quit too. Right, Matt?'

'You punched somebody at Jake's last night,' Dunstan said. He held up a hand as Taggert made to speak. 'I know. The bum started it. But only after you got into an argument over what he'd said at your trial.'

'He lied then, he was still lyin' last night.'

'You've got the whole town jumping and I'm damn sick of it, Kurt.'

'You're sick of it? Man, if you ever spent thirty days straight in the hole at Yuma then you'd know what getting sick of a thing is really like.'

'I knew I wouldn't be able to talk to you,' Matt snapped. 'Tessa, I want this man to quit town. Do you have any influence over him you could use?'

'Sorry, Matthew, but he's stubborn beyond me.'

The sheriff of Amatina leaned back in his chair. In back of him a dozen diners were goggle-eyed and straining their ears, hoping to pick up just something being said between the three people whose exact relationship with each other was still Amatina's hottest topic.

Matt was unaware of everything but Tessa and Kurt and the memories they all shared. He still loved her even though he knew she would never love him again. He could live with that. But there were things he would never lose no matter what.

'All right,' he said to Taggert as he rose. 'All I'll tell you, Kurt, is that you've been warned. You're fraying the edges of law and order here and testing my patience, and I don't allow that in my town. Think over what I just said, for the next time you cause trouble it will be you and me. Nice seeing you, Tessa.'

He was gone.

The crowd seemed disappointed.

Kurt called for the check and they went outside, where life moved sluggishly through Amatina, and the maids at the hotel across the street were drawing the upstairs blinds against the sun.

'I hope that didn't spoil your day, Kurt?'

'No chance. Matter of fact this day's just getting started for me.'

'For you? Not us?'

'Sorry, honey. But last night at Jake's, before I socked that boozer, I heard about some weird guy with a limp who's just come back to Poor Town after being away a spell. I'll try and get to see you tonight.'

'But, Kurt, don't you know the brigade are camped just out at the mine and that some of them are in town today, asking questions about you and Gene, behaving strangely. Surely you can see the trouble signs . . .'

She broke off. He'd left her with a reassuring grin and was now nimbly stepping his way through the horse and wagon traffic, heading for the shady side of town. She watched his tall figure disappear and when she turned she saw a man in militia rig leaning against a lamppost nearby watching her keenly while servicing his buck teeth with a combination toothpick and pipe-cleaner.

Tessa shot the fellow one of her best ice-cold stares and swung off along the walk with a swish of taffeta. The commander's man whistled softly as he watched her go.

*

Sunlight shimmered on the T-2 ranchyard.

Gene finished grooming the white's silky coat, then looked up to see that the girl had appeared on the porch. He wrapped his gear in a worn leather pouch, closed the corral gate and headed across the yard, eyes perfunctorily surveying the surrounds as he walked.

He could see Dobbs at the barn and Bo Treece pitching hay in the loft. Everyone was keeping sharp and would remain that way until certain the danger had really gone.

The girl greeted him with a smile. She still appeared pale, as was to be expected. But her father was much improved and the mother was in the galley fixing a breakfast-lunch for all hands. Things could be a lot worse.

He halted with one boot on the bottom step and the girl saw him in a different light from those times he'd visited the Sheepherder's. She'd always considered him very handsome but somehow too serious for a man of his age. Up here in the Black Rocks surrounded by horses, cows and friends he appeared younger and easier. She saw him as he had become over the years, tall and broad across the shoulders with a tumble of heavy yellow hair and a reassuring certainty in his manner.

In turn he was looking at a girl who appeared to have fully recovered from the ugly things that had befallen the family two days earlier. Namely, an unscheduled visit by 'the hero of Brandaman Valley', Commander Oliver Brogan.

'Everything OK?' he asked.

'Papa is swearing. That means he feels much better.'

'Ever fed a dogie?' She shook her head and he grinned. 'Good time to try.'

There wasn't a lot to learn about feeding a weaning calf. You half-filled a bucket with milk, sank your hand in it then gave the hungry dogie a finger to suck. As he sucked he swallowed some milk, and eventually realized that the finger wasn't necessary and you had yourself a weaned calf.

She smiled for the first time since he'd first sighted her waiting at the doc's for her father to have his broken arm set in plaster as a result of Brogan's visit to her village.

He had a notion of what had taken place but had waited until she'd recovered from the ordeal to get the story straight, and now looked like the right time.

He asked; she told him.

Two days ago the sleepy village found itself invaded without warning by a squad of militiamen led by Commander Brogan. It seemed the brigade had been some twenty-four hours in the Diablo region, and from what she understood, had been considering a raid on T-2 ranch or else were hoping to catch Gene riding to or from the spread.

The brigade were low on supplies and proceeded to take what they wanted, virtually at gunpoint. A pair of them had attempted to molest the girl, her father intervened and Brogan himself had ridden him down, causing his injury. Several other sheepmen had been less severely injured. The last of the

119

invaders hadn't left until night, taking with them food, wine and several slaughtered lambs to sustain them on their journey back north.

Gene's face was blank as she fell silent but inside he was raging.

What he'd encountered at Amatina made two things crystal clear. One, Kurt's release from prison had been like a red rag to a bull for Brogan, who plainly believed his brother's presence there might jeopardize the town's bid for the town patent upon which so many of Brogan's personal and commercial plans depended. The second was that the one-time major driving force in the valley had deteriorated alarmingly in recent times.

That Brogan had actually ventured into the region, to spy on him, or worse, made Gene realize that the he was so obsessed with Diablo now that the danger to himself, the boys and Kurt just couldn't be discounted.

It didn't help to reflect that there'd always been conflict between Diablo and the commander.

Yet he still felt something was missing from the jigsaw. He could understand Brogan hating their guts, but surely there had to be something more driving him to such extreme lengths either to harm them or take them right out of the game?

But what?

The thought jolted into his mind; something connected with Kurt's frame-up, maybe?

'Maybe,' he murmured. He nodded. 'Could be . . .'

'Señor Diablo. . . ?'

He grinned. She'd always called him that. 'Gene,' he said. He sobered as he took her by the arm and they headed back for the house. 'Anything else? Anything they said or did that maybe we should know?'

She frowned in concentration.

'I think they must have done something terrible. I heard some of them talking, one was the evil-faced *hombre* with the thin mustache . . .'

'Trask.'

'Yes, Trask. Well, I heard him say that they should not have hanged some man. That if it became known there could be trouble with the sheriff or the marshal.'

'Uh huh. Did they say where they were heading when they left?'

'They spoke of a place called Medusa mine.'

'Just up the road from Amatina,' he muttered.

He was walking slow but thinking fast as they approached the crowded front porch where the mother and father sat being served breakfast by Dobbs, sporting a huge calico apron.

By the time they got there he knew what must be done.

It took a half-hour to convince the *paisanos* they must remain at the spread where they would be perfectly safe. The drive crew from the south had been afforded fine hospitality during their stopover and proved ready and willing to take care of the T-2 and the family during the five's absence.

They were going back to Amatina.

Genie couldn't give an estimate on how long

they'd be away. His objective was to get to his brother before something bad happened to him then try and persuade him to quit and return to the south with them. But as to what might be expected from a strangely remote Matt Dunstan and an increasingly unpredictable Brogan, there was no telling. All he could do was guarantee his return, along with their safety here. But they must agree to remain at the ranch for safety's sake.

The mother seemed agreeable but the father shook his sorry head.

'No, we cannot leave the sheep. By the time we returned they would be all gone – lost, strayed, stolen – gone!'

'Let 'em go back, Gene,' put in Ramble, anxious to get riding, scenting excitement. 'Brogan's gone. Why should he come back?'

'They're staying.' Gene watched Bo and Eli leading the horses from the stables. He was thinking fast. The solution suggested itself, but it caused him to balk. He glanced sideways at Ramble before clearing his throat. 'OK . . . OK . . .'

His voice faded. Everybody was staring at him. Gene Taggert was never hesitant.

'What?' Ramble prompted impatiently.

Gene looked at the sheepman. 'You . . . you can bring your sheep here to the spread.'

'Sheep!' Ramble's gasp was more like a choke. 'Here? On T-2?'

They would be twenty miles up along the trail before four outraged cattlemen would stop their griping. But they were the least of Gene Taggert's troubles. The closer they drew to Amatina the uneasier he felt.

'Make way, make way, damnit!' Deputy Lomax shouted, ploughing his way through the crowd. 'Come on, come on, you think this is some kind of side-show? Devine, if they won't move, then make 'em!'

Deputy Devine swung his billy club and towners began to scatter from the lawmen's path opening up an avenue through which Matt Dunstan approached the funeral parlor, grim-faced, tight-lipped, speaking to nobody – nothing like the Matt Dunstan they knew.

'Who done it, Sheriff?' a red-faced man in a hard-hitter hat yelled above the clamor. 'Who'd have done that to old Wild Bob?'

'How do we know it was him?' countered another. 'Ain't no identifyin' what Old Mose brung in, I can tell you that for free.'

'Get out of the way!' Devine snapped at the citizen, prodding him in the short ribs. He turned and beckoned his superior who strode past him without a glance to enter the gloomy interior of Valley Funerals.

The lawman paused to allow his eyes to adjust to the gloom. He removed his hat and turned to stare at the laying-out bench where the undertaker and woodcutter Old Mose had deposited the corpse the oldster had brought in off the Whipple Plains just that morning.

'Sheriff,' the undertaker murmured, but

Dunstan didn't seem to hear. His eyes were focused on the dead man. He winced as he stepped closer. He had dodgers on Wild Bob Killane at the jailhouse although what time, decomposition and the buzzards had done to this one made sight identification impossible.

'Did he have anything on him?' he asked.

The undertaker indicated a small pile of belongings on a nearby bench and Dunstan turned to examine them.

'He was hangin', Shurf,' the woodcutter supplied. 'Bin there for days by the looks. Damndest thing I ever saw. We ain't gone through this stuff yet.'

'Any tracks?' Dunstan asked, picking up a worn billfold.

'Some. Quite a few now I come to think of it. Lynch mob, I guess.'

'Name on this, Sheriff,' said the undertaker. 'Take a gander.'

Dunstan studied the wallet. 'Robert Killane . . . Wild Bob all right.'

He figured the dead man to have been around five-ten, slight build and sandy-haired, which tallied with the dodger's description of Wild Bob Killane. Wanted: bank-robbery, kidnap, smuggling and attempted murder. Estimated age: 45 years. No known family. Former associate of Charlie Taggert of Diablo, now deceased.

He looked up to see Lomax studying at him closely.

'What?' he snapped.

The deputy shrugged awkwardly. 'Nothin'. Just wonderin', Sheriff.'

'Wondering what?'

'Well, you know . . . Brogan's been carryin' on about Diablo and suchlike, how the Taggerts are the devil's sidekicks and such . . . and the brigade has been round and about plenty the last week or so . . .'

His voice trailed away. Considering the sheriff's dour mood the past couple of weeks Lomax almost expected anger or at least a curt reproof for speculating. He drew neither. Dunstan simply set down the wallet, snapped, 'Bury him, council expense,' and walked out, seeming not even to see the crowd as he headed back for the law office.

It was some time before the undertaker emerged to inform them that the mutilated body was indeed that of the former Wild Bob. Only then did the militiaman at the back of the mob go to his horse and ride from town along the north trail to the old Medusa mine.

CHAPTER 9

THE CRIPPLED MAN

'Storch?' queried the bum. He shook his head. 'Dunno nobody by that name, mister,' he insisted.

'This is Tin Can Lane?'

'Sure is, but—'

'Then you should know him,' Kurt Taggert insisted. He broke off as three ragged urchins came pelting through the twilight with a drunken deadbeat wielding a stave in hot pursuit.

'Varmints! Thieves!' the drunk was bawling, slipping and sliding in the refuse that was all a part of Poor Town streets. 'I'll teach you to thieve my meths!'

Taggert's nose crinkled. This wasn't his first visit to the shady side of town. Crabtree Alley, where the murder of a man named Clanton had taken place a decade earlier, linked the back streets of Uptown with Poor Town. In his search for leads or

126

clues connected with a matter ten years in the past, he'd lost count of the numbers of brawls, arguments and brushes with the sheriff he'd survived, but hadn't eased off once. In truth, he'd stepped up his efforts over the past week. He felt time might be running out on him.

Nobody even remotely connected with his case was in any way eager either to talk or offer anything much that might be of help. Several times he'd told himself he'd checked out every man with a limp in the entire valley, yet they kept on turning up. Like Storch. He'd heard the name several times during his investigations, but was convinced the Poor Towner had either quit the valley or had died. But just last night he'd spoken with a derelict who insisted the man was back, limp and all.

Now he was standing in the street where the man was supposed to have lived on and off most of his life, and he wasn't about to be fobbed off.

'He's got a limp,' he persisted, as the clamour of the pursuit subsided. 'He's a loner, they say, and mebbe a little crazy—'

'Crazy Emil?' the bum asked, rheumy eyes widening.

'Well, yeah, I hear that's what he's called. You know him then?'

'Sure.' The man pointed. 'The shanty with the hessian flap hangin' down. That's it. I thought he'd gone for keeps when he upped and disappeared a few weeks back, but he showed up again just yesterday. But don't tell him I said nothin', mister, on account he is one scary kind of varmint. They named him good that one, real good.'

Kurt's jaw muscles worked as he pressed a coin into a grimy palm and moved off. It might be nothing, yet he'd felt his heart pick up a beat when he heard that Storch had apparently vanished two weeks ago. That would coincide with his own arrival in town, he calculated. Might Crazy Emil have some reason for wanting to avoid him, or was he just desperate enough to be clutching at straws?

Only one way to find out.

Watched curiously by urchins, nodding drunks and slatternly women leaning in their doorways, he approached the lean-to. He didn't hesitate but strode straight through the entrance flap.

A tall man was seated at a table spooning juice from a can of peaches into his mouth. The can dropped and the man cursed as he lunged for the knife on the sideboard, snake fast despite the hindrance of a severe limp.

'Take it easy, damnit!' Taggert yelled, bringing the side of his hand down hard on a scrawny arm to jolt the knife from the man's grasp. Bearded and wild-eyed, the man threw a wild blow. Kurt went under it and pistoned a fist to the guts. Storch buckled over his arm and collapsed to the earthen floor.

'So what's got you so proddy, pilgrim?' Kurt panted, as his eyes grew accustomed to the deepening gloom. He'd seen the limp, the man's violent reaction. What else was there to be found here in this Tin Can Lane's bachelor quarters?

He began to search. Everything was old, junky, piled up in corners or hanging from the pole rafters amongst the spiders. Voices sounded outside. He ignored them. Much of the stuff he was uncovering seemed pretty suspicious, empty wallets or purses, trinkets and personal effects and faded documents that seemed unrelated to this man or his lowly position in life.

Storch groaned and stirred, began dry-retching. Kurt continued examining junk piles and old crates that might not have been disturbed in years, dust floating in the air, the barking of a couple of dogs now adding to the clamour outside.

He shook the cracked leather bag and was about to cast it aside as empty when he realized it had more weight than he'd at first thought. He opened it and reached in, his hand closing over a rusted six-shooter.

'Bastard!' croaked the man sprawled in the dirt and junk. Then he hollered, 'Thief. Help. I'm bein' robbed. Help!'

Unhurriedly, Kurt toted the weapon to the entrance, thrusting it suddenly at the group of neighbours closing in warily. They jumped back, shoving one another aside in their fright. Kurt didn't see. He was studying the metal base plate of the piece intently by the last dregs of daylight where a skilled hand, obviously a smith, had etched the initials K.C.

His lips moved: 'Kyle Clanton?'

Trying to rise on hands and knees, Storch began foaming at the jaws like he was having some kind of fit. Out on Tin Can Lane, somebody was hollering for the law.

'Hey! Who do you think you're shovin', lady? Oh, it's you, Miss McNair. Didn't recognize you. Hey, you jokers, lady wants to get through.'

'Thank you,' Tessa panted, and the citizen tipped his hat with one hand and assisted her to make her way through the crowd with the other.

Up on the law-office porch, Deputy Lomax stood with boots widespread and a Winchester angled across his hips as she mounted the steps.

He grimaced. 'What are you doin' here, Miss Tessa? This ain't any place for a lady, or for all these gawkers and nosers neither for that matter. Get back there, Leroy Tubbs, or I swear I'll put a round between your big boots! But you'd better leave too, Miss Tessa – hey, Miss Tessa, you can't go in there!'

Too late.

Tessa had slipped through the partly opened front door in the blink of an eye to emerge into the bright lights of the jailhouse's spacious front office, which had been so very familiar to her a long time ago when she and the sheriff of Amatina had been lovers.

The two men standing facing across the lamplit desk turned their heads to stare, Dunstan's expression one of tight-lipped anger, Kurt Taggert's more one of alarm.

'Tess!' he said, coming to take her hands. 'You shouldn't be here.'

130

'Is what I hear true, Kurt?' she replied. Her quick look took in the blocky shape of Deputy Devine standing guard over the rear door and the cells where a sick-looking man sat slumped on a bunk. 'You've uncovered evidence linking some-one to the Clanton killing. . . ?' She paused to indi-cate the shabby prisoner. 'Is . . . is that him?'

'Do you mind, Tessa?' Dunstan said, angrily, coming round the desk. 'Damnit, woman, this is a critical situation and—'

'And I'm quite sure you're doing everything in your power to help Kurt clear his name . . . as you haven't always done these past weeks. Have you, Matthew?'

It was suddenly very quiet in the Amatina law office. Tessa had spoken quite calmly yet there was a sharp edge to her voice. While she and Matt Dunstan had maintained a relatively easy relation-ship – for ex-lovers – their conversation had rarely touched on the Taggerts or other controversial matters such as the commander or the recent lynching of outlaw Wild Bob Killane.

But now she was plainly reminding the lawman of his duty while casting some doubt on how he had been exercising that same duty as far as Kurt Taggert was concerned.

That hit Matt Dunstan hard even if he did manage to conceal it.

'Do you have some reason for coming here this way, Tessa?' he asked stiffly. 'In the middle of a very serious discussion?'

Tessa's poise was impressive as she glanced

calmly from one face to another, before stepping lightly past the sheriff to pick up the heavy Colt revolver lying there.

'So, this is the gun.' She looked at Kurt.' Where did they say you found it?'

'You phrased that correctly,' Dunstan said, curtly, taking the weapon from her. 'Where did they say this thing came from? Nobody saw it happen. Storch claims he never seen it before in his life. What I'm trying to establish here, despite the interruptions, is whether this weapon was found in Mr Storch's home, or perhaps was located where someone else may have concealed it ten years ago.'

'You know damn well I'm telling the truth, Matt!' Kurt said, angrily. 'First person to enter that shack after I went in, was Devine here. I showed him the bag . . . he saw how I'd torn that dump to pieces searching. What more do you want?'

'The man's right, Sheriff,' the deputy weighed in. 'Anyway, when Storch came around he was bleatin' "I never killed him. . . I never killed him . . ." even though nobody had mentioned Clanton up until then. Then there's the fact that Storch admits he disappeared for two weeks after Kurt came back, which looks to me like he was scared of facing him, of maybe being found out.'

'I don't recollect inviting you on to the witness stand, mister.' Dunstan was sarcastic, angry at last. 'Just shut up, Devine, just simply shut your mouth. Hear?'

Nobody spoke for a long moment after that.

Everybody stared at Matt Dunstan as though seeing a stranger. For a man with one of the coolest heads in Amatina, the sheriff seemed to be looking, acting and sounding like someone losing his grip.

This dramatic switch of character seemed particularly alarming to both Kurt and Tessa, who knew Dunstan better than anybody. It was like seeing an old friend – and he was still that to both – beginning to come apart before your eyes.

Kurt Taggert was riled by the treatment he'd received yet he appeared more sad than anything. Sad and dismayed that Matt Dunstan seemed hell bent on letting down the office he'd always managed with such class.

Lomax appeared in the doorway, alarmed by the sudden quiet. Relieved to find everybody just standing there trading stares, the man said quietly, 'Better come have a word with the mob, Sheriff. Everyone's saying we've caught Clanton's real killer and that Kurt shouldn't have ever have gone to jail – that sort of stuff. You're the only one who can quiet them at times like this.'

Dunstan sighed. 'All right . . . damnit!'

'What about Kurt, Sheriff?' queried Devine.' Is he free to go?'

'For the time being – I guess.' Matt's eyes were glittering from something deep down inside that should have stayed hidden as they flicked from Kurt to Tessa and back to Kurt. 'Both of you can leave.' He paused, then added sourly, 'Together.' He raised a hand imperiously. 'But don't you quit

FIVE GUNS FROM DIABLO

town, Taggert. This affair is a long way from over.
You mightn't be out of the woods yet.'

Time seemed to drift as Kurt calmly rolled a
cigarette and lit it. He shook out the match. He'd
reached for calm and found it. 'You're the sheriff,
Matt,' he said, taking a pale Tessa by the elbow. He
paused in the doorway. 'Notice I didn't say "you're
the law"?'

Dunstan said nothing, made no sound, but his
emotions swirled through the room like smoke.

The lights of the Palace saloon and hotel blazed a
welcome, and Gene Taggert was first out of the
saddle as his travel-stained riders clattered up to
the crowded hitch rail. The Palace had always been
the brothers' favoured watering-hole before, and a
towner had just told him Kurt was inside right now
– celebrating.

Celebrating what?

He led the way up the steps and through the
batwings. At the bar, Kurt whirled as if he knew it
was them coming through even though there was
no possible way he could have done so.

'Kid!'

'Old-timer!'

The crowd of slick gamblers and fallen doves,
chuck-a-luck callers and sunburned teamsters, the
whole winners-and-losers cross-section of Amatina
night life stopped what they were doing and just
grinned at the way the two tall brothers hugged
and slammed one another on the back, amazed at
such a display affection between two relatively

hard-nosed characters.

Truth of it was, Gene and Kurt were taken a little by surprise themselves. Yet the warmth was genuine tonight if for no other reason than that both had been exposed to danger during their separation and were happy to see one another all in one piece.

But there was also a second reason, and the bartender set up a fresh round while the Diablo five learned for the first time about the day's events involving Kurt, an old six-shooter and one Poor Towner named Crazy Emil whom Kurt was insisting should be charged with the murder of Kyle Clanton.

Gene gulped down a schooner of beer and wondered where all his anger and tension had gone. Sure, he had work to be done up here, but the very genuine probability that Kurt may have uncovered the real killer and might therefore expect to get the thing he wanted most – a clean name – overshadowed everything else.

He ordered another round. Kurt slapped him on the back and, when things began to calm, Gene related events as they'd occurred down valley involving the militia and the sheep farmers.

The general mood sobered as Kurt digested the fresh news on the militia, then went on to apprise the five of the lynching of one-time Diablo identity Wild Bob, along with the widening suspicion that Brogan might have been responsible.

'Most folks believe they done it,' insisted the eavesdropping barman. 'Brogan, that is. One of his boys was in here last night, and he said the commander always hated Wild Bob's guts on account he come from Diablo, and that he swung him up when he caught him because he never got to swing you, Kurt.' His brow puckered. 'You reckon he might be goin' loco like some say?'

The Diablo bunch hefted their glasses and moved to a table out of earshot. They stayed there an hour, some of the talk serious, but most of it not. The five had come north fearing trouble of one brand or another, but instead had been greeted with good news. It was hard not just to sit back and enjoy a rare good time, which was what they were doing when the batwings swung inwards and Deputy Lomax entered and headed their way.

'Trouble?' Gene asked his brother.

'Mebbe not,' Kurt answered. 'Seems the deputies can't wait to rack Storch up before a judge and jury, but Matt? Well, if Matt's happy he's doing a fine job of hiding it.' He nodded a greeting. 'Hi, Deputy. What you drinkin'?'

Lomax, solid and boyish, grinned.

'Another time, I reckon, Kurt.' He sobered. 'You got a minute?'

'Sure,' Kurt said, rising. 'What you want?'

'The sheriff would like to see you. He's over at the First Chance right now.' He put on a grin when he saw the other's scowl. 'It's OK, he's cooled off. Seems in a good mood, in truth. What do you say?'

'Sure, I'll talk to Matt any time. Want to come, Gene?'

'Er, not this time,' Lomax said. 'The sheriff said this is private. Real private. OK?'

'Hell, man . . . OK! Lead the way.'

With every passing minute counted out by the skinny black hands of the ancient barroom clock, Kurt Taggert's prison-toughened face grew more and more sombre.

He hadn't known what to expect from his first one-on-one opportunity to sit down with his one-time friend, but it certainly wasn't what he was hearing.

'Let me see if I've got this straight, Matt,' he broke in. 'You say you are offering me a chance to avoid trouble by dropping this charge against Storch and . . . and getting gone? I have got it straight, haven't I?'

'Straight as a gun barrel.'

'You're loco!'

'Listen, Kurt. You're a man with a record. You've stirred up this town no end since you got paroled and you've trodden on some big corns—'

'Like Brogan's?'

'His and others. But he's gunning for you, Kurt, and there's no way he's about to sit back and watch you try and reverse the findings of your trial which you know would will cast reflections on all of us . . . the judge, the commander, myself. With the decision on the town patent upcoming any time now, we can't allow your case to be revived and splattered across the whole territory. Can't you understand that, Kurt?'

Taggert rose, stony-faced, and dropped notes on the table top.

'I'm, payin', Matt. It was worth the cost to find out just where we stand. You're no friend. Forget Tessa, she's got nothing to do with this. This is you and me, Matt. So next time we cross, be careful. They taught me good in Yuma how to deal with phoney double-dealing snakes!'

'Kurt!'

Heads turned at Dunstan's angry shout, but Kurt Taggert was already gone. It was late when Lomax and Devine halted across the street from the old church. They stood gazing up at the long narrow windows and the bell tower that never rang anymore.

The sheriff's quarters lay in darkness. That was mostly the case these nights although the deputies were anything but sure the boss was sleeping following his parley with Kurt Taggert. There were many things they neither knew nor understood about Matt Dunstan these days, yet until just a few short weeks ago they felt they'd known the man as well as a couple of dedicated young deputy sheriffs could know any superior, any place.

Around them the town seemed quiet, but to their practised ears the atmosphere didn't seem genuine. Following the incident in Poor Town backed up by the developments at the jailhouse involving Dunstan, Kurt Taggert and Tessa McNair, it seemed that Amatina should be jittery tonight as it pondered on where all this could lead, how the Militia might react, and the return of Gene

Taggert and his pards – a dozen uncertainties.

Or maybe the edginess and uncertainty were centred closer to home for Deputies Jud Lomax and Cole Devine as they finally turned away from the church and made their slow way along Main for the Drumhead.

Lomax caught Devine glancing at him sideways – just as the other had caught Devine a few minutes before.

They stopped and stared at one another; close friends, straight-edge lawmen and protégés any sheriff could be proud of. But why were they so edgy tonight? Why were they looking almost guilty as they stood searching for answers in one another's faces.

Finally Lomax said, 'You reckon we done the right thing?'

'Look, we agreed we had to, so what—?'

'I know we agreed. But that was then. We were both for it then. But things sure changed fast afterwards. First we had Kurt Taggert braggin' that he was goin' to call for a new trial and a judicial review of the old one. Next thing the boys from Diablo rode in lookin' all fired up either to ruckus or celebrate. Then the sheriff meets up with Kurt and afterwards straightaway drops from sight. Somehow all that makes it feel now like we did somethin' we might regret, that we moved too fast.'

Devine turned his head to stare back at the church. Had he glimpsed the silhouette of a man at a window, staring down? He shrugged and swore softly.

'Look, we did it because we reckoned it was the right thing – that we had no choice. Let's leave it at that, huh?'

'Whatever you say, Deputy.'

'No. Whatever *we* say, Cole. This was something we both agreed on and we're both stickin' to it, right or wrong. Right?'

Devine grinned. 'Right, of course. Come on, nothin' like a double shot to quiet a man's conscience my daddy always used to say.'

'You said you never had a daddy.'

'That makes me either a bastard or a liar.'

'That's OK. Sometimes I feel like that's the only two kinds we have in this town.'

The spectacle of the commander in his quarters resembled a magic lantern show where the mechanism was winding down leaving the pictures still flickering but slowing in a way that made you want to yell at the operator either to adjust it or give you back your ten cents.

But Trask had seen Brogan's weird lapses before. They had been far more frequent recently than at any time in all the years he'd ridden at the leader's side. Trask knew Brogan would come back from that scary place he visited in his head eventually at times like this, maybe come back even stronger and more authoritative than ever to tell them exactly what they should do and how it should be done.

So the waiting dragged on and the lamplight in the big Sibley tent that was the commander's HQ

140

while on operations, cast the shadows of the three men present hugely on the canvas walls and roof.

The militiaman who'd brought the latest bad news from Amatina stood with his weight on one leg holding his hat while hatchet-faced Trask stood by patiently fingering his black moustache.

The commander tracked the sluggish progress of a moth across his desk blotter with a forefinger that gave the labouring insect a prod whenever it stopped.

Brogan's eyes were blank, his breathing uneven and laboured. He'd been swaggering around the table reliving the excitement of their recent sweep down the valley when the scout returned. He'd immediately lapsed into one of his 'blanks' as Trask termed them, and that had been a full half-hour ago.

During that time twenty heavily armed men paced restlessly about outside beneath the beetling brow of Medusa's shaft-head. They were speculating on how Brogan might react to the news concerning Kurt Taggert and the startling discovery he was said to have made regarding his murder case.

Even the new recruits in the militia had come to understand the depths of Brogan's obsession with the Diablo riders during their expedition to that region. The old hands were predicting Brogan would simply not permit a reopening of the Clanton case, but were uncertain as to just what action he might be prepared to take to shut it down. Most of the new fish were hoping that whatever it was it would lead to action, their recent campaign having whetted their appetites for it. For they were, no matter what uniforms they wore or ranks they laid claim to, basically hard men without conscience who'd do anything the leader ordered.

Trask was pouring branch water from a metal canteen when Brogan suddenly spoke.

'All in town you say, mister?'

Trask grinned. Brogan looked normal, sounded it.

'Yeah, that's the report, Commander. Kurt Taggert and the five back from Diablo. Seems the bunch were pretty sore about what happened when we were d—'

'Checked in at Buck's Trailhouse, that right?'

'Right.'

Brogan began to move round the Sibley, leather creaking, bearded jaw slowly lifting.

'And riling Dunstan?'

Trask grinned broadly. The man had heard everything. He'd just acted like he had turned strange, was all.

'So Miller says, Commander.'

Brogan locked hands behind his back. 'Trailhouse on the edge of town, vulnerable, not much room there for anybody but that dog pack. And we've got a force of twenty-three veterans just salivating for action after the ... er ... disappointment of down valley.' He looked at the other keenly. 'There is a time in the affairs of men when destiny lies in the balance. Agreed, Trask?'

'If you're thinkin' what I think you are, Commander, don't you consider that could be goin' a tad too far? I mean, what about Dunstan and—?'

'I can handle Dunstan.'

'If you say so, sir.'

'I know so. He won't interfere and neither will that chicken-livered town. As for afterwards . . . we were simply carrying out our duties as officially authorized vigilantes in undertaking a task that the law or the army are plainly incapable of handling.' His fierce eye blazed. 'Correct?'

Trask was relaxed. Fighting was his stock in trade. 'Reckon so, Commander.'

'Then what the devil are you waiting for, man? Is the troop assembled?'

'Commander. . . ?'

Brogan was suddenly fully upright, clear of eye and imperious of bearing as he tugged down his rumpled tunic and snapped his ceremonial sword scabbard hard against his knee boots.

'Full operation formation, damnit, sir. We're ridding our county-capital-to-be of all pestilential outlaw scum immediately and once and for all. See to it!'

'Yes sir, Commander. At the double, sir.'

CHAPTER 10

THE SIEGE

Johnny Ramble couldn't sleep.

For a man who'd danced and drunk until midnight in the bar below then spent an hour or more on the balcony with his pards and Kurt's beautiful woman, talking over old times, swapping jokes and just simply enjoying the bunch all together again just like old times, he should be sleeping like a log.

Instead he found himself seated on the edge of his bed in his Levis, massaging the back of his neck the way he often did back home or on the trail when he sensed something wasn't exactly as it was supposed to be.

He eventually quit rubbing his neck and jumped to his feet with nerve ends jangling. That was it! That was what had awakened him. That old famil-

FIVE GUNS FROM DIABLO

iar feeling . . . goddamnit!

His Colt was in his fist as he went swiftly to the window. He looked out. Nothing. The littered rear yard of the trailhouse lay innocently silent in pale moonlight, trees and open country beyond. Everything was hushed and still, just the way it should be at God knew what time in the morning.

He went back to bed and lay staring at the ceiling.

The hell with it! A man might as well be up as trying to fool himself he was going to drop off. Maybe someone else was suffering the wide-awakes. Maybe they could get a game going.

Fully dressed the Diablo rider quit his room and made for the lobby. From the corridor he saw there was just one turned-low lamp at the desk but it cast enough light to see by without straining the eyes.

He was about to enter the lobby when Buck's front door whispered open.

He didn't know what made him stop. Maybe it was the stealthy way the door eased inwards, or maybe he was thinking of that twitchy feeling that had first awakened him.

A man entered the carpeted lobby without a sound. He was toting a rifle and wore the butter-nut-colored jacket of Brogan's Brigade!

Ramble was backing up when a second figure entered and cut his gaze directly towards the corridor. He was seen. The rifle jerked up.

'Freeze, Ramble, you bastard. You're under

arrest. Lift 'em and be quiet if you know what's good—'

Ramble drew and cocked twin Colts faster than the eye could follow.

'Drop them guns, boys. You're what you call trespassin'. Get shook of 'em!'

The first man did as ordered. The second didn't. Instead he jerked the rifle violently upwards almost to reach firing-level before Johnny Ramble squeezed trigger.

The rifle went one way and the man the other. Clutching his shoulder in agony he cannoned into the other brigadier and both went crashing to the floor as the doors burst fully open and a squad of brigadiers came rushing through with guns roaring insanely.

But the Diablo man was no longer there. He was tearing back along the corridor kicking every door he passed to arouse the entire floor. Instinct told him this was the big one, the day many said would never come. But somehow Johnny Ramble had always known it must.

'Get down!' Gene roared as a bullet droned through the shattered window and slammed hard into the ceiling, showering him with plaster. 'Someone's on the balcony. Dobbs, can you see what . . .'

His voice was swallowed by a volley of fire from the barn across the way where Brogan was pacing to and fro in the smoky gloom directing the battle and inspiring his men like the commander of old.

Buck's Trailhouse was completely encircled by a ring of spitting fire-flashes.

The volley of fire thudded hard against sun-dried boards of the trailhouse's weathered walls and tore ragged holes through the window shutters, busting the panes and scattering fragments of glass over furnishings and crouching fighters.

'We're going to the galley,' Gene ordered, striding for the door. 'We'll get a better line of fire on the party forted up in the tack room from there. C'mon, Kurt, that means you too.'

'We're better off here.' Kurt's face was sheened with sweat. The siege had been under way for thirty minutes or more and every man was sweating profusely.

He leapt up and drilled a shot through the windows, then dropped again as return fire crashed and rolled. For a long moment he shielded his head with his arms against flying glass; when he looked up he was alone.

'Damnation and dog crap!' he snarled. 'Who's runnin' this outfit anyway?'

The answer was plain; Gene's was the calmest head at Buck's that night. He'd proved it in the way he'd negotiated the release of the other house guests with Brogan earlier while flatly rejecting all demands to surrender. Instead he'd posted the men for maximum effect and then led each successive counter attack against the odds.

He looked cool and acted it. But inside he was raging as Kurt came swinging in to take up his position amongst the pots and pans.

They knew Brogan had been running out of control for weeks, but this was a murderous outrage. The defenders had two men wounded, the town was rocking to the gunfire – and where the hell was Matt Dunstan anyway?

He had every right to want to know the answer to that, but it was some fifteen minutes later before the enemy fire suddenly ceased and an eerie silence fell over the battle scene.

Then the shout: 'Gene! Kurt! It's the sheriff, Hold your fire, I'm coming in.'

The brothers legged it to the front in time to see Dunstan's tall figure walking through the ghostly tendrils of gunsmoke drifting across the face of the barn. His hands were empty and he walked as he always did, without haste and apparently fearless.

Kurt jerked the door open and jumped back. There was no shooting. Moments later Dunstan stood before them removing his hat.

'You boys sure know how to raise hell, don't you?'

The brothers stared. It was a stilted attempt to lighten the moment that fell completely flat.

'Don't crap around, man,' Kurt said roughly. He gestured with a long muscular arm. 'Why the hell ain't you stopped this an hour back? That crazy old bastard is out there tryin' to murder innocent people yet this is the first we've seen of you.'

'I'll do the talking,' Dunstan said with his old authority. He leaned against the desk and turned his hat in his hands. 'This is a real bad situation, boys, I don't have to tell you that. The commander won't listen to reason. I've tried. He's convinced you set up that evidence, believes reviving your case will blacken our name all over and cause us to lose out on the patent to Fremont City.'

'So he comes here to kill us and you stand by?' Gene's voice was cold with anger.

The sheriff straightened.

'This is the deal. Kurt, I can get you and your men safe passage out of here on the understanding that you drop your case and agree to quit the valley and never return – on oath. All of you.'

The brothers gaped incredulously.

'You mean for Kurt to give up his fight to clear his name and . . . and us just lie down and let that mad old bastard bust every law in the book and walk all over us . . . just because you can't or won't do your job, Dunstan? I can't believe what I'm hearing . . .'

'Maybe I can, Gene,' Kurt said grimly. He fixed the lawman with a hard eye. 'Matter of fact, mebbe I see it all now. Like the way you suddenly quit on backing my not guilty plea during my trial . . . then saw me off to Yuma.' He nodded. 'Yeah, that was the point you stopped playing straight, wasn't it, Matt? And we both know why. You figured with me gone you'd have your chance with Tessa. Only it didn't turn out that way, did it? Now this caper. You see a chance to get rid of me forever . . . set me running like a dog for the rest of my life so you can make one more try for her. Why . . . why damn me, man, but you are not any kind of lawman. You are a phony, Matt, mebbe the worst I ever saw!'

The lawman's face was white.

'She was always too good for you, Kurt. She'll see that when you're gone and—'

'He won't be gone,' Gene said grimly. 'None of us will be. We'll whip this old bastard, and we'll see them tear that star off your lapel, Dunstan. Or maybe I should call you Judas.'

Dunstan's face turned ashen. He was a man falling apart before their very eyes, the façade of the hero-lawman he'd worn with such distinction for so long coming down, leaving in its stead a desperate gambler watching his last big plunge go down the chute.

But he wasn't finished. He'd risked too much to lose now.

'All right,' he said woodenly. 'I won't confirm what you've said, but I won't deny it either.' He paused as flames roared hungrily through a hole in the lobby wall. 'I loved her before you and I'll have her even if she doesn't love me – when you're gone, Kurt. Sorry we couldn't do business,' he added and turned as though to leave.

Next instant he whirled and hauled Colt with the speed of a gun wizard as he raged, 'Then you'll all die, damn you!' his twisted face unrecognizable. But even his dazzling, desperate draw was still an instant too slow. For Gene had anticipated him; read the intention in the man's eyes.

His .45 belched fire and flame and Matt Dunstan staggered backwards, gun dropping with a thud and arms hugging himself as though cold before he fell, kicked once and was still.

'Ten minutes!' Brogan hissed, checking his fob watch. 'It's obvious Dunstan has failed us. . . damned weakling. Very well, do it!'

Over the mass of shavings, kindling and pitch pine piled high against the blind end of the trail-house beyond reach of the defender's guns, Trask now splashed the coal-oil from a can, then stepped back.

With cool deliberation, the gunman cracked a match on his thumbnail and dropped it.

The oil-drenched pile exploded into a sheet of flame that leapt up the wall and immediately began chewing at the eaves. Somewhere a woman screamed, 'Fire!' and within the trailhouse's wooden walls grim-faced men reloaded their guns and tried to figure how long it might be now before they would have no option but to come out shooting.

The lobby was choking with smoke. A blazing beam fell from the high ceiling and crashed to the floor near where Johnny Ramble stood with an unlit cigarette between his teeth.

'Ah, just what I needed,' he said, flicked the cigarette through the flames then sucked it into life. 'Nothin' sets a man up like a good smoke, my daddy always said.'

In the hellish light his bleeding, smoke-blackened comrades stared at him wonderingly. In that moment out of hell, Ramble seemed to typify what they were and had always been: defiant, not too serious, but brave enough when the chips were down. It might not have been true, but it was a good self-image to take to the grave with you – and death was surely waiting for them out there.

With grim calm they began to shake hands all round. Gene took his brother's strong grip and their eyes met and held before they silently turned to face the burning doors. Front or rear, it didn't make any difference. They were surrounded, and now the enemy was starting up shooting again, like they couldn't wait for them to show, so eager were they to finish them off.

Then came the yelling.

But it wasn't the same sound of taunting and jeering that had tormented them before as the fire caught hold; it was something different, like men in fear or panic.

Gene stumbled to a bullet-shattered window, At first it proved impossible to penetrate the roiling smoke clouds. Then a gust of wind blew the scene briefly clear and his red-rimmed eyes snapped wide.

He saw a man in brigade butternut stumble and fall to his knees, clutching his chest; in the background was a horseman with a smoking gun wearing a marshal's badge pinned to his vest!

A US marshal?

His brain couldn't take it in.

But surely those two racing riders who suddenly appeared pumping shot after shot into the dim ranks of the enemy were real?

Or were they? Maybe he was seeing things. He

must be.

Another rafter came thundering down before he could react.

'We're goddamned saved!' he bawled at the top of his lungs, wanting desperately to believe it. 'Come on – we're getting the hell out of here!'

He didn't wait for any response. They had to get out. Now! He roared something unintelligible above the roar of the fire and reefed the door open, the heat scorching his fingers. He had a Colt in either hand as he lunged drunkenly across the smoking gallery half-blind and staggering in time to catch the amazing spectacle of three riders, one a marshal and the others troopers in navy blue, hazing two staggering militiamen ahead of them like sheep round the blazing corner of the building.

He swung round to stare in bewilderment at the smoke-grimed faces behind through half-blinded eyes, still not sure if he'd gone crazy and was seeing vivid visions of foolish hope.

He would never forget the way Kurt croaked:

'B'God, that pilgrim on the bay – that's the US Marshal from Canyonville! And he's brought the goddamn military!'

So it was real!

In an instant his vision came clear. He whirled to glimpse the burly figure in brigade butternut rushing for a rearing horse and blasting at a trooper crouched behind an overturned dogcart.

Gene's Peacemaker thundered and the brigadier died running.

He was the last man to fall before a bloodied Abel Trask staggered from the barn waving his white silk shirt over his head.

Amatina was still in shock.

Gene Taggert saw it and felt it as he stood on the front porch of Midge Riddle's, drinking coffee with Marshal Thompson and the deputies. It could hardly be otherwise, he thought, as he gazed southwards at the smoke tendrils still drifting above the ruins of what had been Buck's Trailhouse.

But Amatina would recover. This wasn't just a platitude but a reality, for it was a rugged community, no stranger to adversity. Overnight it had witnessed a bloody siege, the death of its sheriff and an eleventh-hour rescue by the law in the shape of Marshal Thompson, four deputies and the several young troopers he'd seconded from the fort.

It had also witnessed the final curtain call for Commander Brogan.

He glanced in the opposite direction where the doctor's room stood on the Medusa Street corner. Brogan was over there and had been ever since Trask's surrender signalled the end of the gun battle. The commander had been staring at the same spot on the wall for the past five hours. Doc Blinx had diagnosed a massive stroke brought on by overexertion and rage but mostly by shock, an irreversible condition which meant he would most likely be deemed unfit to stand trial over his final outrage that had brought him down.

The deputies shook hands with Thompson and nodded to Gene as they moved off. Devine and Lomax walked with both pride and relief today, for it had been they who had gone over Matt Dunstan's head and wired for the marshal when their lawmen's instincts warned that Amatina was rushing towards disaster.

Today it had come and gone, and for the first time in twenty-four hours Gene Taggert finally found himself thinking yearningly of home, of Diablo, the T-2 and a girl he might persuade to help him forget any of this had ever happened.

The tall marshal enquired if he felt like eating yet. 'Some solid chow and a good long talk, maybe?' as the man put it.

He was surprised to realize that he felt like both.

A big blustery rainstorm was blowing in across the valley from the north on the day of the meeting called by Thompson at the council chambers after allowing time for the dust to settle. And for Amatina to begin at least to adjust to the most tumultuous events in its history and not, to pay, so much attention to the gaping black hole where the trailhouse had stood on the quiet side of town.

The federal marshal had made it plain it was to be a general meeting only today, not a judicial hearing, and certainly nobody was slated for trial, as yet.

Something violent and shocking had taken place here and it was the marshal's belief that only

FIVE GUNS FROM DIABLO

by studying and understanding the circumstances leading up to the siege and the breakdown of law and order could such a holocaust be avoided in the future.

Just about everybody of consequence was there, including Judge Pooley, who announced he was already at work preparing for Storch's trial, following the man's full confession. He was also reviewing the transcripts of Kurt Taggert's case in the hope of discovering just where and how the law had managed to get it wrong, a timely move considering that an eventual judicial investigation was very much on Thompson's own agenda.

A handful of chastened militiamen survivors were also in attendance. The general sentiment appeared to be that the ex-brigadiers might escape heavy penalties on account of the almost hypnotic power Brogan had wielded over them all in his role as a driven manipulator of events, whose influence had corrupted simple men and turned them into dangerous men, without conscience.

The local population was swollen by dignitaries fighting for seating space with all the newspaper reporters and numbers of visiting judges and magistrates from the north with their retinues. The big airy room was crowded and Gene Taggert considered himself lucky to get a window seat with a sweeping view of the valley and the approaching storm. He felt he might get to day-dream through it all here without attracting attention.

He knew it was all as important as well-fitted skivvies, and that Amatina needed first to know then get to understand what had befallen it.

But he already knew all he needed to know.

His brother's trial and conviction had been orchestrated by a Taggert-hating Brogan who had used his power and influence to intimidate the presiding judge and secure Matt Dunstan's complicity. A fearful Trask had revealed all this already and was prepared to swear to it in a court of law in the hope of saving his own hide.

Emil Storch had also accepted advice that open confession might prove his only way to dodge the noose, admitting to the robbery-murder of which Kurt Taggert had been accused.

Gene reflected that in all these evil events only Dunstan had been motivated by love, even if it had been love of a hopeless, twisted kind.

As for the rest, well, he was content to sit there and let all the words, speeches, breast-beatings, explanations, regrets and glowing word pictures of the future just flow over him while he focused now on what was really important to Gene Taggert, namely getting home and resuming life on the T-2.

Late afternoon found him preparing to do just that. Both he and Kurt had supplied sworn testimony concerning Matt Dunstan's actions and admissions, while his patched-up boys had all furnished the gathering with their accounts of events leading up to and encompassing the siege of Buck's Trailhouse. They would be leaving on the understanding that Thompson might call on them when and if further hearings and investigations should transpire.

Gene was saddled up and ready to ride when he realized Kurt and Tessa seemed to be disagreeing about something over by their buckboard.

He walked across with a grin.

'Hey, you're not married yet. No wrangling until after the wedding.'

'I'm afraid I'm having second thoughts about visiting, Gene,' Tessa said. 'I've just realized we may be there for some time, and I'd be the only woman on the place.'

'Not so,' Gene said as the boys came strolling across, leading their horses. 'Not even Kurt knows it yet but there's not one but two women on T-2 and—'

'And that ain't all that's awaitin' us,' cut in a sober Johnny Ramble. 'You want to tell your brother or will we, Gene?'

'Well, heck,' Gene said, ' I don't know what—'

'What are we talking about?' Kurt demanded suspiciously.

'Sheep.'

Gene didn't know if Ramble alone dropped the ugly word or if all four hissed it in unison. But the effect was dramatic. His brother went white.

'Sheep? What do you mean – sheep?'

'All over the place,' Dobbs answered grimly.

'A farm-full of sheep,' insisted Bo Treece. 'Far as the eye can see. Sheep on cattle land.'

'Sacred cattle land,' put in Carlaw, going one better.

His brother's dropped curse was Gene Taggert's

cue to swing a leg over his cayuse and move on out. He could see it wouldn't be all smooth sailing for the Taggert brothers, back on T-2 together again for the first time in years. But then it never had been.

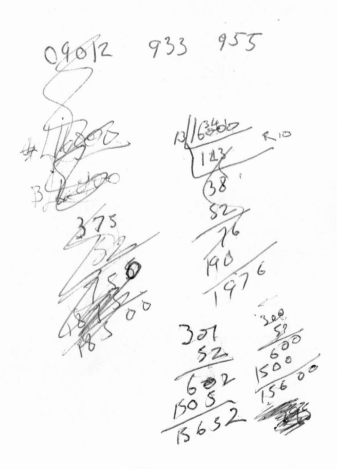